The Cuckoo Baby

Edited by M J Grant

Joseph Sage was born in 1946. He began his career early, relating short stories in school and college and later publishing a volume of these under the title 'Pearls of the Sages'. His great interest in psychology and philosophy influences all his writing. An experienced world traveller, he has left his mark on people of many cultures, changing their outlook so that they better understand the world, their societies and their environments.

www.bookpearls.me.uk

The Cuckoo Baby

by

Joseph Sage

Dolphin Press

Published by Dolphin Press
www.bookpearls.me.uk

Copyright © Joseph Sage 2005

ISBN: 0-9549743-0-1 UK

Printed and bound in Turkey by Karaca Offset +90.252.212 95 27

For my daughters Ephat,
Dina and Shelley and for Bedri

With gratitude to Marilyn for her
help and support

PROLOGUE

Now I stood in the middle of the hospital nursery surrounded by babies mostly only a few hours old. Without stopping to consider further, I picked up the sharply pointed scissors and stood between two of the babies. My body was shivering even though the temperature outside was over 35°C.

The soft breathing of the babies was magnified increasingly loudly in my ears, like the warning beat of a jungle drum. I had been in that room many times before, but had never been so conscious of the distinct smell of warm, unweaned infants, mixed with the sharp cleanliness of disinfectant and sterilising solution. The whimpering of one or two babies sounded shrill over the flat bass tones already reverberating through the room. Each tiny bundle seemed hardly to occupy any space at all, swaddled as it was in a maass of white linen, lying barely noticeable at one end of a small transparent crib on wheels. Only the little pink face or mass of dark hair that topped each bundle gave any indication that it was not just a carefully rolled piece of material.

With heightened awareness my brain absorbed every detail of the room. On one wall was a half open cupboard housing tidy piles of linen and nappies. In the corner stood the night nurse's desk, on which she had left a neat stack of patients' notes and some bottles of glucose solution. And there, above the desk on the shelf, was prominently displayed the important implement that I needed. I looked around quickly and listened to make sure that no one was nearby.

Swiftly I loosened the blanket and gently lifted the arm of one baby, which was encircled by a plastic identity bracelet. Cutting off the bracelet, it took me no more than a moment to slip the typed name label from the damaged bracelet and put it into a new one. I felt agitation throughout my body. My hand was shaking. Worried that in this state I might hurt the delicate wrist of the second baby, I forced myself to control the shaking whilst I cut through his bracelet too. Now, instead of the trembling, my heart thumped so hard I feared it would overbalance me. All fingers and thumbs this time, it seemed to take an eternity to put the old label into a new bracelet. With my five senses on alert, I took from the shelf the implement which was used to seal the identity tags and clipped the bracelets with their changed identities round the babies' wrists.

'Good luck. Be rich,' my eyes swam with tears as I gave my baby Danny a last kiss, 'I'll always love you,' I whispered, choking.

By now I was more than keen to be gone, but my luck took a final hand and my eye was caught by the blue patients' notes, reminding me to swap the cardboard cradle labels as well. This I did, not allowing my eyes for one instant to leave the door. Quickly I replaced the instrument and scissors on the shelf and put the damaged bracelets in my pocket. Shaking all over from fright and apprehension, I left the nursery and went to the ladies cloakroom to recover.

****

Hurrying back to my bed a few minutes later, I made sure that the rich lady in the next bed was still asleep. Like a chick hiding safely in the comfort of its mother's feathery bosom, I snuggled tightly into the warm protection of the blankets, feeling secure that not a soul had seen me.

For a long while I lay there, brushing the cold sweat from my forehead and my thick black hair. It was a colour one rarely saw, standing out like polished coal, its intense blackness highlighting shades of red and brown.

'Crow' they called me when I was a child; I hated it. Now that I was nearing thirty, they called me 'the Arabian princess', for my hair accentuated lively green eyes, a delicate olive complexion and finely chiselled features, and my long willowy legs and gently curvaceous body gave a graceful flow to my movements.

Sure now that no one had seen me, I sat up in bed and made myself comfortable.

'Ruth,' the head nurse's efficient voice called me from the other end of the ward, 'Can you keep an eye on Josephine and let me know when she wakes?' she asked amiably.

There in the bed next to mine, Josephine, the rich lady, was still lying heavy and motionless after the exertions of a difficult labour. She had arrived only yesterday, with two dainty but expensive suitcases, which a smartly liveried chauffeur carried for her into the room.

'My dear,' she had said with an air of confidence, 'I have five sons and this time I am having a girl and only a girl.' Her manner had told me that her money usually got her what she wanted.

Her blonde hair had been fashionably set in the most youthful style, as if she had just stepped out from beneath the brushes of an army of hairdressers. Her large lustrous eyes had been emphasised by careful makeup and her skin had bloomed without the faintest trace of a wrinkle. The owner of a large hotel in the centre of town, although she neglected to mention which, she had professed fiery socialist principles, giving them as the reason she had not taken a private room. Even so, she seemed to find no contradiction in sending her children to the best private schools, indulging them in all the luxuries they could want and she could afford.

'Oh no, not again. It's a boy? True?' a feeble voice, like the rustle of a page turning, issued from the bed next to mine.

Josephine now was ashen-faced and dishevelled. Her eyes were surrounded by a network of fine lines, and wrinkles creased her forehead and chin. Her hair hung lank and damp, in places matted to her head, and her breasts were large and drooping beneath her thin hospital nightgown.

'Yes, a boy,' I answered, consoling her, 'and he's sweet and beautiful.' My eyebrows involuntarily rose an inch as I grew suddenly fearful that Josephine would ask me how I knew and discover what I had done. But for the moment she was too weak and upset to notice.

'That's it, no more,' Josephine stated resignedly, 'I wanted a girl so badly, but you see Ruth, I have another boy – the sixth.'

This time, anxious not to repeat my mistake, I answered carefully, 'I always wanted a son so I could call him Danny.'

'Son?' she queried in astonishment. 'Boys are not easy to bring up, my dear.' Josephine struggled to raise herself into a comfortable position in bed. Her supreme confidence in the face of her own disappointment made me more than ever aware of the contrast between her life and mine and I decided to tell her what life is really about.

'You see I don't come from this area,' 'I announced, 'I come from Hopetown. I moved here with my husband Jack when we got married.'

'Hopetown?' a puzzled frown passed across Josephine's face as she searched her memory. 'That's near Spring Hill, and near the best part of the capital, is it not?' she ascertained.

'I suppose you could say that,' I sighed with no conviction, 'but to me it could've been a million miles away. You see, the public utilities you'd expect to serve every home in a modern town didn't reach the house where I lived. We didn't have any electricity and the water we did have by some miracle, came from a tap outside in the yard.

I say 'the house' but you probably wouldn't call it that, because it was nearly falling down. In some rooms there was only half a ceiling, where it had either fallen away with age or had been smashed. An attempt had been made to cover the gaps with large pieces of wood and sheets of corrugated zinc, but you could still see the sky through the holes that were left. The only stable thing about the house was its walls, which were made from blocks of quarried stone.

Our toilet was in a shed outside at the back. It didn't have a proper door, just a flexible cover made from canvas. Inside, flat on the floor, providing the facility, was a wooden slat with a hole in it, which rested over a manhole. And that place was our shower as well. There was nowhere else to wash. We used to fetch cold water from the tap outside in a battered tin bucket. The bucket had such a jagged edge it was only sheer luck it didn't cause anybody a nasty injury. I had to wash my body and my hair with plain household soap.'

'What, kitchen soap?' Josephine interrupted, her mouth falling open, 'You used that on your beautiful skin?'

I nodded in affirmation.

'I am the oldest of five children. My father was almost constantly drunk. He never held a job or even looked for one, being the kind of person who believed that he couldn't alter what fate had set out for him, so there was little point in trying.

It was my mother who had to support us. She worked morning, noon and night, scrubbing other people's floors and doing other people's dirty washing. I remember when I was very small, tramping around with her, knocking on door after door asking if anyone wanted any washing done.

As soon as I was old enough, I took on her responsibilities at home, having to look after my father as well as my brother and sisters. Because of that I often missed school. Even so I never gave up hope that one day my life would change.'

Josephine stared at me, her dark blue eyes were wide but unfathomable. 'Dear God,' she almost whispered, 'Did people really live like that?'

She was so sympathetic that I felt inclined to tell her that I had changed my son for hers to give him a chance, but I did not dare.

'So you came here to better yourself?' Josephine prompted.

'That's right. Here I hoped to live in a place where you didn't see beggars and thieves and drunks and whores everywhere you went.'

'But you said Danny. Why Danny? Is he Danny's son?'

'No, no, I wish he was! It's a long story.'

'It's all right, Ruth,' Josephine's voice reflected compassion, 'We have all the time in the world to gossip. Do tell me about it, please.'

'Very well,' I assented resolutely. I took a deep breath and transported myself slowly back in time. The lovely scents and the evocative sounds of a most special day vividly replayed themselves in my mind and I seemed to be back in the yard of my ramshackle home.

It all began in the springtime when I was 16 years old. I had completed my final task of the day, washing the battered tin plates in the outdoor tub and I was free to indulge in my favourite occupation. I sat down and tilted my face upwards to receive the warm soothing caresses of the afternoon sun. I half closed my eyes and was carried into a wonderful world of fantasy. My daydreams gave me tremendous pleasure and all the satisfaction I could not hope for in reality. Like Cinderella, I was rescued from my miserable existence by a brave and handsome young man, but he did not have to be a prince, I was quite happy inventing someone who would dance away with me in his strong arms to somewhere brightly lit and exciting.

The dream had so immersed me as to become almost real. Gradually in a hazy vision I became aware of a young man in uniform passing in front of me. I raised my eyelids slightly, thinking that he was part of my fantasy.

He stood before me, majestic and strong, suffused with an extraordinary shiny glow. Here indeed was the handsome prince who had come to sweep me off my feet.

"Can you see your fortune in the sun?" a friendly voice penetrated my daydream.

Slowly I lowered my head, opened my eyes wide for a moment but quickly shut them again. The young man was wearing unusually smart khaki and the brilliance of the brass decoration on his cap glinting like burnished gold in the sunlight blinded me. The soldier moved and his shadow fell on me. I smiled, thinking how strange that fate should send a prince in the guise of a soldier and opened my eyes gently.

"If you have finished your washing up, could I dry the plates for you?" he asked warmly. His voice invaded my consciousness so that I could not ignore him.

"Thank you, it's nice of you to offer, but it's not really necessary. The sun does that job for me," I said, giving him my full attention.

He smiled, his gorgeous blue eyes lighting up and dazzling me, "Sometimes it isn't sunny. If you'll give me your permission, I'll come then and dry your dishes for you."

He spoke to me politely, with clarity and in a cultured accent, displaying perfect manners, which told me that our neighbourhood did not match his. I felt shy and terribly embarrassed by the circumstances in which he found me.

"You don't sound like you come from round here. How can you be here in those moments when the sun has gone?" I said brightly.

"For a beautiful girl like you, I would fly to the moon."

The soldier grinned again. His smile was like a thousand flowers suddenly bursting into bloom.

Now the sun could not be blamed for causing the burning in my cheeks. The handsome soldier ceased looking at me and some of my high colour subsided.

"May I have your permission to sit here on this stone?" he pointed to a large piece of rock nearby.

"This isn't a place for you to sit," I giggled shyly, worried that he might dirty his lovely uniform.

"I am old enough to know what I want," he said confidently, making me feel that even if it were the most unsuitable place on earth he would sit there just to be next to me.

I was overcome with embarrassment. Instinctively I rose onto my slender legs intending to run into the house to prevent this nice young man being disappointed when he found out how thin I was.

"Don't go!" his voice restrained me, "I stopped to talk to you because you are beautiful and slender and I like slim beautiful girls."

How did he know what I was thinking? I was so amazed that I turned round and smiled at him self-consciously, wondering what else he knew.

"Will you be kind and show me where the bus stop is? I do not come from this neighbourhood and don't know my way about," he asked, immediately putting me at ease.

"Yes, it's there," I pointed in the direction of the bus stop and somehow we started walking towards it together.

"I am an officer in the army," he said, "and I came here to find one of my soldiers who lives in this area and hasn't returned to the camp. Before reporting him missing to the military police, I wanted to know the reasons for his absence. I knew he came from this vicinity where the residents often live in hardship."

All the time he spoke, the soldier used the most refined language, never resorting to common expressions, which would have been likely to upset me. He described my terrible area delicately, shunning vulgar terms like swindler or whore. I walked next to him, listening to him give a clear appreciation of our problems and feeling that I had found the only man who could understand my situation.

"Did you find the soldier?" I turned to him and our eyes met for the first time.

"Yes, I did," he looked at me intently, "But when I saw how he lived, I promised to arrange an interview with people who can help him, if he reports back for duty by tonight. He said he would do what his officer asks."

12

I was more impressed with every minute that passed by his caring and understanding attitude and began to pray that he would stay, but all too soon we reached the bus stop.

"My name is Danny," the charming soldier volunteered.

'Oh, that's why Danny!' Josephine exclaimed enthusiastically.

Impervious to Josephine, I sat for a moment in silent contemplation. Unbidden, a huge tear formed under my eyelids.

'Ruth dear, are you all right?' Josephine looked concerned at my unguarded display of emotion.

I wiped away the tear and took a deep breath.

'Mmm,' I murmured, 'Danny was so special.' I leant back on my propped pillow and renewed my concentration.

'Danny asked me if I had seen the new film, *The Longest Day*, which everyone had been raving about. "Will you allow me the pleasure of taking you with me to see it?" he asked.

My pulse raced. Did I hear correctly? Was he asking me? I knew nothing about the film, but I did know that more than anything else I wanted to see him again. I agreed readily.

"Thank you, your assent makes me very happy," Danny bent his head jauntily to one side and treated me once again to his dazzling smile, "Now I'll meet you in the city centre …" he stopped in mid-sentence and looked at me closely. I had just begun to wonder how I could get into town without the fare for the bus. "No, that won't do," he continued, "I don't think it will be safe to leave a beautiful girl like you to reach the cinema alone. There's a strong possibility I might lose you to someone else on the way. I will meet you right here by this bus stop," he whispered.

Once more Danny had anticipated me. Danny's solution was typical of the care and chivalry I came to know was inherent in his nature. Danny never let me down.

Up until that time my wish to stay with him longer had been granted, for even though a few buses had already come and gone, he had stood firmly next to me, not appearing to notice them. I knew that I ought to have drawn his attention to them, but my heart resolutely refused to let my voice speak and I could not summon the strength to overrule it and wilfully separate from him.

But as soon as we had made our arrangements, I began to wish that the next bus would come quickly so that he could go without having a chance to change his mind about meeting me. I also wanted enough time to wash myself before the sun went down and to choose the best of my three dresses to wear.

The bus came and without saying more, I parted from him, already sustaining the hope that I had indeed found the prince I had longed for.

I ran all the way home and immediately fetched the old tin bucket. I filled it with water and carried it to the horrible toilet to have a shower. I took off my old dress and hung it over a hook on the wall. I was so happy that my grim surroundings and the conditions I was obliged to suffer did not affect me as they usually did whenever I entered that place. My whole being was gripped by excitement, longing for the moment when I would once again meet my prince and I could think of nothing else. For the first time, I did not feel the chill of cold water as it splashed on my skin. My brain was so completely consumed by the thrill of anticipation that it had no capacity left to give the usual feelings to my muscles. The unpleasant sensations thus blotted out, my only awareness was of an enjoyable shower cleansing all my problems from my body. The large empty can of tomato puree, which we used to rinse ourselves, might well have been a porcelain jug and the unrefined grey household soap, which we used for every cleaning task, could just as easily have been the whitest, creamiest and most exquisitely perfumed toilet soap.

I finished my shower and pausing only to retrieve my dress from the wall, in no time had reached the bedroom in which stood four iron bedsteads. Each one supported a dilapidated mattress, over which were thrown a strange collection of blankets, woven mats, sheets and patchwork covers. There were mattresses under the beds too, enough to accommodate all the family. But there were no cupboards or any kind of furniture in which to hang clothing. Instead, our clothes and other meagre belongings were kept in wooden boxes, one or two for each of us, which we recognised by the treasured possessions they contained.

When the heavy rains came, we were obliged to wear the clothes in which we stood. Any alternatives had been soaked, for periods of time ranging from a few hours to several days, depending upon when the sun next made an appearance. For the most part we were fortunate and the sun shone immediately, giving us a chance to spread the boxes and all their contents under its warm drying rays, quickly evaporating the water they had absorbed. The sheer volume of rainwater caused it to accumulate in large pools and find its way into the boxes by slithering through the doorways, under the walls and along the clay floor. Surprisingly, very little rain penetrated the house via the incomplete ceilings so that the damage was confined to damp clothing.

But on that lovely day these problems did not matter to me. I lifted my remaining three dresses carefully out of my box and laid them on the mattress, savouring every moment of my exceptional preparations, even though my decision had already been made. I selected a deep blue cotton dress, which, since it had only been passed down to me six months previously, was my latest acquisition and merited being called my best dress. I put it on just before my mother came in from work.

My mother was tall, almost two metres in height and as thin as a stick. The thinness was probably the way nature had made her, but I always harboured the suspicion that it was because of the hard life she had led. She had also always seemed old to me but that too was probably because she had no opportunity to look after herself. Dowdiness had set upon her early in life, she had not seen even one new dress since the day she was married.

She did not need a mother's intuition to see how happy and carefree I had become, unlike my usual quiet or dreamy self. My cheeks had a rosy hue and my eyes sparkled, in fact I could feel a wonderful vitality radiating from my whole being. She was the first member of my family I had seen since meeting Danny and I wanted to run over to her to take her as my partner in a joyful dance around the room. But my mother's questioning look and down to earth manner stopped me.

"Where are you going?" she asked.

I needed only half of this excuse to tell her everything that had happened to me that afternoon. I thought she would be as excited as I was, but her face took on a preoccupied, slightly worried expression and she said only, "Well I do hope that you won't be disappointed. Will you make an effort please to come home straight after the film?"

I nodded hard, replying, "OK, Mummy".

Her worried look faded as she asked me, "Have you got any small change for the bus?"

"I don't need any. Danny is coming to meet me here at our bus stop."

"I am glad," she looked much brighter, "He sounds like a good boy, but even so, you must take some money in case by accident you lose Danny. You don't want to be left without the means to get home by yourself."

My mother went into the kitchen where she kept a few spare coins in a cracked china cup for emergencies. I followed her and she gave me enough money for the bus journey home.

Now that I was ready and all my arrangements had been completed, I grew suddenly nervous that I might be late and miss my exciting rendezvous. I grabbed a slice of bread, already spread with jam, from the middle of our rickety wooden table. Shouting goodbye as I left the house, I attempted to eat it, but could not swallow. I was so nervous and happy, the bread was not important. I just wanted to be with Danny.

Some little birds were hopping about near my path searching for food. I gladly scattered my bread to the lovely creatures who never failed to brighten my days and hurried in the direction of the bus stop, hoping that I was not late.

My heart missed a beat when I arrived at the bus stop and Danny was already there.

"I'm so sorry I'm late," I apologised. We had no proper clock in the house and I had no idea of the correct time.

"You're not late at all, in fact you are early, but I've been waiting for you for half an hour," he reassured me.

That was Danny, honest to a fault and in consequence completely trustworthy.

My spirits soared into the clouds, thrilled in the knowledge that he had so looked forward to going out with me, he had come as early as possible to wait for me. I felt warm all over and my cheeks highlighted a colourful blush. My dream was coming to life in all its detail, only the real feelings were far more intense and satisfying than the imaginary ones.

It was such a wonderful pleasure to feel really wanted after having been certain for so long that only an imaginary man would ever notice me.

On the bus Danny started to tell me about the army, especially about the regiment in which he served. The insignia he wore showed that he was attached to a forward fighting battalion. He described in detail the badge of each different rank of soldier in the army and with every word he spoke I learnt something new.

I no longer wanted to go to the cinema, by the time we reached our destination. I would have been more content just to find a corner where we could sit and talk and be alone together undisturbed. I was learning a great deal and enjoying Danny's company so much that I felt it would be a waste of our time together to watch someone else's story when we had each other to discover. But I knew that Danny was keen to see the film and we joined the queue for tickets.

"I don't think it is right for people to talk loudly in the middle of the film," Danny explained, once we were seated inside the plush red velvet-decorated auditorium. "If you would like me to explain anything about the film, I shall have to put my mouth very close to your ear to whisper to you. Of course, I won't be able to do that without putting my arm around the back of your chair. Will you allow me to do that?"

"Yes, of course," I answered, thinking that he really had no need to explain.

"I love gentle girls and I asked you out because I could tell at once that you are gentle and shy. But I don't feel that I can take it for granted that you will be happy about my behaviour without asking you first." Again Danny showed me his consideration and thoughtfulness.

The lights came up at the interval and Danny asked me if I had understood all the film.

"Nearly all. Yes, I understood nearly all of it," I muttered, unable to tell Danny that much of the film, particularly the humour, had gone over my head.

Danny leaned nearer to me, put his head close to mine and explained everything I had not been able to follow. I was amazed to discover how well he understood me, knowing exactly which sequences had been difficult for me to comprehend. Danny's careful explanation gave me a good idea why the rest of the audience had laughed.

In the second half I had the benefit of Danny's quiet appreciation of the role of each actor in his part. I was impressed by Danny's knowledge of the film and the type of characters it portrayed, but I was impressed more by Danny's abiding caring manner.

At the end of the performance, Danny told me that I must wait in my seat until everybody else had gone, because he did not want anybody to push or squash me.

Outside the air was cool and fresh and we began walking along a brightly lit shopping street. Unmistakably the smell of warm doughnuts reached my nostrils, wafted on a cushion of air from a nearby shop. I did not stop or look specially in the window, even though my mind had often dwelt on doughnuts, but Danny turned to me perceptively, "I know what you are thinking about, Ruth," he said.

I looked at him questioningly.

"You didn't know that I was a magician and mind reader, did you?" Danny gently teased me. He waved his arms and bowed with a theatrical flourish, "Hocus pocus, magic spell, I can see, do … do … dough nuts. Here they are sitting right in front of you dusted with fine white sugar."

How does he know? I wondered.

"But I can see something else … … an empty stomach, and I can see some juicy meat cooking over an open fire. Now the meat is sitting on a plate accompanied by fresh salads and hot potatoes. A tall glass dripping with sparkling condensation and filled with ice cold beer is standing next to the plate."

Danny's voice returned to normal, "Now you must decide whether you want the juicy meat and salads or the doughnuts which I saw so clearly in your thoughts. I am not such a brilliant mind reader that I can tell what your decision will be."

My heart was filled with emotion. At last, someone really understood me. Tears welled up in my eyes, but I managed to forestall them and smile gratefully. I did not answer though, for I did not know what to say and could not have uttered a word, even had I wanted to.

Danny's expression melted. On impulse he put his arms around me and cuddled me affectionately. Then he took my arm and led me to a restaurant.

Candles flickered invitingly on the intimate table set for two. Danny ordered for me, saying he would secure something befitting a sensitive stomach. The waiter soon returned with two plates. On one rested a large steak which I was certain was too much and too tough for me. I need not have worried. He set that plate before Danny and gave me a dish of chicken with boiled potatoes. Another waiter brought a huge plate of different salads and pitta bread.

I waited for Danny to start, uncertain how to tackle the food, but he said he was waiting for me first. I attempted to cut the mouth-watering food. My jacket was uncomfortable, tight and ill fitting. I struggled for a moment and decided to take it off. Before I could pull at the sleeve, Danny leapt to his feet, stood behind me and helped me to remove it.

Danny was already my perfect gentleman, but the minute it took for him to carry my jacket to the coat peg near the cashier, I knew that he was truly my prince. He was determined to spoil me from start to finish, for he had saved a special treat for after that delicious meal. Hand in hand we strolled along the main street, joining the happy throng of young people who had come out to enjoy the evening air.

Our footsteps took us in the direction of the doughnut shop, but to my surprise, the formerly delicious smell had virtually lost its temptation. Nonetheless, Danny ordered us a steaming hot confection each. I bit carefully into the delicacy I had long desired and dreamed about. It tasted wonderful, but after all my longing, tonight the taste was enough for me. I just did not have enough room to finish it.

"You must make the effort to eat it and give yourself the chance to grow a little stronger," Danny tried to convince me.

I made a great effort and managed to eat half of the doughnut. Danny saw me struggling and took the other half from me, swallowing it in one go.

I giggled self-consciously, feeling sorry that I had let him down when he had been so good to me. Danny reassured me with a hand on my back, "Don't worry, I understand you."

Indeed he did. Danny's arm around me made me feel totally safe. Who could hurt me when I was under his protection?

Danny and I made our way to the bus station. The bus stood with its driver already seated and its doors open, seeming to beckon any would be passengers to enter.

"Danny, you'll be tired tomorrow, it's very late and you have to start very early. Please leave me here, I can go home on my own," I implored. Though I didn't really want to go at all, I remembered that I had promised my mother.

"If you think I'm going to let you go home by yourself at this hour of the night, or is it the morning," he said, looking at his watch, "You really, really think I'm silly."

I wanted to pay for myself, but Danny gave me no opportunity. He just shovelled me up onto the bus in front of him. He flashed a card at the driver and paid for one only, following me and sitting next to me.

"What is that card?" I asked, voicing the question that had bothered me before, "Why didn't you pay for two?"

"My father is a driver with this company and that makes him a member of the transport cooperative. As his son, I have the right to travel free anywhere I choose," he explained.

"How lucky you are to be able to travel like that, anywhere you fancy, any time you want!" I enthused. It sounded so exciting.

"Ah, unfortunately this luck has come without the chance to take advantage of it. Before I was busy studying and now the army takes up almost all of my time. When I reach 19 next month, I will lose the card and the right to free travel."

Next to my home Danny pointed at the stone he had sat upon earlier.

"If I could find a suitable chain," Danny suggested, "I could hang that stone around my neck and keep it as my good luck charm close to me forever."

How happy I was at the thought of such devotion.

Danny held me very close to him and for the first time kissed me, a sweet, lingering kiss that sent little thrills through me, wanting him never to stop.

"I did not kiss you before in case you didn't want me to and you would have had nowhere to run to," he explained.

He need not have worried except that I would have clung to him too tightly all evening. I felt for the first time a deep longing to keep another human being close to me and to stay locked in his warm embrace for all of the dark, lonely night.

Too soon the embracing circle of Danny's arms was loosened.

"I'll come to see you soon," he said and began walking away.

My heart stood still when I realised we had made no arrangement to meet again. I stepped forward to call him, but Danny turned round before I could utter a sound.

"I don't know when I'll get my next leave and I don't want to make an arrangement I may not be able to keep," he said.

"Oh, please Danny, can we make an arrangement now, I'd prefer that, even if you can't make it later."

"All right, let's say in four days time, but I will come sooner if I can. As long as you won't be too upset if I have to rearrange it," Danny agreed.

With that he turned and walked away. My eyes were fixed on him, noticing for the first time the slight curl of the hair on the back of his head as it was picked out by the light of the moon.

That night my excitement and sense of the wonder of Danny transported me on a tide of fantastic dreams. I found myself floating with my prince in cascades of sunshine and everlasting happiness. In the morning the excitement lingered to carry me through the long, seemingly interminable wait until I could see Danny again.

I was awoken by the cockerel that belonged to our neighbour. Every morning his piercing crowing upset me, waking me up to my miserable life, but today his call sounded like a wonderful song. I quickly rose from my mattress on the floor and pushing aside the old piece of heavy curtain that served as a door, went out into the yard. The cockerel was a striking bird, big and strong and seeming to have been painted all the colours of the rainbow. All day he would strut about like an aristocrat, showing off his glorious plumage. Now I saw him standing erect and stately on the neighbour's gate, where he usually stood to call his daily reveille.

"Good morning my lovely friend," I said sweetly, "Thank you for waking me up on this beautiful day."

The rooster fell silent, looking at me. Every morning he was ready for me to throw a slipper or a shoe at him to stop him crowing and send him elsewhere. Today he did not have to stop crowing or fly away.

"Call again, call again, I love your voice," I urged gently and somehow he understood and began crowing again and preening his feathers between each call.

As I went back inside the house I met my mother. She saw my smiling face and cuddled me affectionately.

"You look happy," she remarked.

I told her everything that had occurred the previous night. My mother listened attentively to my story, but her face took on a pensive, almost wistful expression.

"Please darling, don't get too excited or expect too much. Life is full of surprises and sometimes there are disappointments too."

I did not know what she meant, though I realised she was trying to warn me about something. Nevertheless, I dismissed her words, as I knew that Danny would never deliberately do anything to hurt me.

My daily tasks began with getting my brother and sisters ready to go to school. My mother had already gone to work and although on that day I had no enthusiasm for any jobs, it was my duty to help my mother, who was obliged to work cleaning other people's houses and taking in washing. For this hard labour and long hours, she earned only a pittance and then lost most of it to my father who, even though he could barely stand up on his two feet, somehow always contrived to appropriate the money to buy drink.

The younger children regularly wet their beds and each day there were bound to be several smelly, urine-soaked mattresses. I picked them up from the firm clay floor, which was flattened and hardened from years of feet pressing it down, and carried them out into the yard to dry in the sun. Even my 15-year old brother Jonathan was not immune to this unfortunate habit. Over the years my mother had tried every known remedy to prevent bed wetting, from strong herbs to magic, but to no avail. All that was left to us was the hope that nature herself would intervene and stop him.

'Yes, I had that problem once with one of my boys, but thankfully it didn't last that long. He stopped of his own accord,' Josephine interrupted me rather condescendingly.

For every minute of every day, whatever tasks I performed, I longed for Danny to come to see me again. Then suddenly, unexpectedly, a day before arranged, but nonetheless three whole days after our first meeting, I heard a voice calling me.

"Ruth!"

It sounded like Danny's voice. I thought my imagination, with all my yearning for Danny, was playing tricks on me and took no notice.

"Ruth!" the voice came from behind me.

I turned round and stared hard in the direction from which the voice seemed to originate, anxious to catch sight of my prince, but could not see anyone.

"Ruth!"

At last I located the sound of his voice coming from behind the wall near where the cockerel usually sat. Just then Danny jumped over the wall as easily as the cockerel flew over it. My heart leapt too.

"What are you doing here?" I asked in surprise, running to him and hugging him.

"I am off duty for a few hours, so I came to make sure that no other soldier was chatting to you."

I was so pleased to see Danny that I had momentarily forgotten the mattresses. However, their pungent odour did not allow me to forget them for long.

'I flushed the colour of beetroot when I realised that the mattresses' pungent odour was assaulting Danny's nose as well as my own. But like the prince and protector he was to me, Danny bestowed the same concern and regard on the rest of my family. Danny jumped on to one of the mattresses, using it like a trampoline, as if finding it there was the most natural thing in the world.

'What! Ugh! He jumped on the soiled mattresses?' Josephine exclaimed, horrified.

"I'm sorry about the ...," I began, attempting to apologise for the unpleasant smell and dilapidated condition of the mattresses.

"How old is the one wetting the bed? Who does this mattress belong to?" Danny interrupted me, still jumping.

"The youngest one," I answered quickly, unwilling to reveal the real culprit.

"You know, I wet my bed until I was eleven," he revealed this intimate information in such a matter of fact way that I gained the confidence to tell him the truth about Jonathan. "If I see your brother, I am sure that I will be able to help him to stop wetting the bed ever again."

Danny did not know how hard we had tried before and my first reaction was to think that it would be impossible, but then, of course, I remembered that my prince could do anything.

"It will be very nice if you can!" I said.

We sat down together in silence for a few minutes, inclining our faces towards the morning sun. As we sat like that, so close to one another, I felt a wonderful spell had been cast over us. He must have felt it too for presently he said, "I want to kiss you, but I don't think that this is the right place. I don't want the neighbours to get the wrong impression of you."

I wanted him so much to kiss me and would have liked to invite him into the house, but was fearful lest the moment he saw the appalling state of its interior, he would leave and never return to me again. Even though my instinct told me that Danny was not the kind of person to be affected by such things, I was not willing to put him to the test.

Instead we sat and chatted. Danny told me a story.

"There once was a poor man who had a wife and five children. They all lived in a tiny hut, no bigger than a shed and it was always very crowded. Fed up with his life, the man went to see his religious leader.

'I can't bear it any more. The place is tiny. There's no room to do anything. It smells. I want to kill myself. I've had enough. Will you give me permission to kill myself?'

'Oh,' said the religious leader, 'We can't give you permission to commit suicide so quickly. First you must pass a test.'

'Surely I've done that already. My life is hell,' the man continued complaining bitterly.

' All right, all right! Do you keep any animals?'

'Well, yes, I've got a goat.'

'What you must do is to go home and bring the goat to live in the house with you for two weeks. At the end of that time, come back and see me and I will give you permission to commit suicide,' the religious leader instructed.

'What!' the man protested loudly.

'You must do exactly as I tell you, if you want justification for your action.'

In a hopeless state, the man returned to the hovel and did exactly as he had been instructed. The goat was brought to live in the hut and in no time the family's terrible existence worsened a hundredfold. The goat smelled. It relieved itself everywhere. It ate the children's clothes and tore the furnishings. Nothing in the house was safe from its destructive habits.

'Get that animal out of here,' the man's wife shouted, but he refused, keeping his secret to himself.

Two weeks passed. An hour before the deadline, the man was waiting to talk to the religious leader.

'I've had enough. I can't take another second more,' he shouted at the religious leader as soon as he appeared.

'Yes, I quite agree. You must go straight home and take the goat out of the house. Then come back in another two weeks and I promise I will give you the permission you seek.'

The man hurried home and immediately ejected the goat from the hut.

Two weeks passed, but the man did not reappear before the religious leader. Three weeks passed. At the end of four weeks, the religious leader met the man in the street.

'I've been waiting for you to return to me for your permission to commit suicide. I am ready for you now.'

'Thank you very much,' said the man, 'but we've got lots of room, the place doesn't smell and all our clothes are intact. My life is so good now, I don't need it.'"

The story was so entertaining that I forgot the time. Far too soon, my brother Jonathan arrived home from school.

"Hello Jonathan! Danny meet Jonathan," I introduced them.

Is it really time to make the children lunch? I thought, wondering how the morning had passed so quickly. Perhaps Jonathan had been released early.

"Jonathan what's the time?" I asked.

"I don't know the time, but I finished school as usual, so it must be about the usual time," he replied.

Danny looked at his wrist, but realised that he had not put his watch on.

"Perhaps you should go indoors to see what the time is?" he asked me pleasantly.

Jonathan laughed heartily.

"Why are you laughing," Danny's brow furrowed slightly though he remained smiling.

"We've had loads of clocks in the house, but you never find one that tells the right time. Every one was thrown out by someone who found out it didn't work properly. We find the sun is more reliable. You can tell the time from its position, you know," Jonathan explained.

"I've been trying for ages to use the sun as my clock," it was Danny's turn to laugh, "It would help me in the army, but I've never managed to get the hang of it."

All this talk about time reminded me again that the other children would be home soon and would be hungry.

"Please will you excuse me Danny, I have to go and make something ready for the children to eat."

"You don't have to," Danny stopped me, "Do you like kebab in pitta?"

"We've never had that, but people say it's nice," Jonathan answered for me.

"What time will the children be here?" Danny asked.

"They'll be here any minute," I advised.

Danny nodded sagely as if registering important information.

"I think I can help you to stop wetting the bed,' he turned to Jonathan, addressing him straightforwardly.

Jonathan's face flushed and he pursed his lips in a way that I knew meant he was fighting back the tears.

"You know I wetted my bed until I was sixteen," Danny continued rapidly.

Hearing this Jonathan smiled awkwardly, showing a sign of relief.

"We tried all the tricks in the world, but nothing could help me," Danny revealed, "Until one night I had a dream that I was with my friends in the woods and we were having a contest to see who could urinate the furthest. Just at the moment when it was my turn, something must have disturbed me. I woke up from the dream and found myself wetting the bed," Danny paused and looked Jonathan straight in the eye, "Do you have those kind of dreams? Do you play those kind of games with your friends?"

"Yes," Jonathan replied wide eyed, his expression plainly showing that he was wondering how Danny knew, "Yes, I do."

"Sometimes I dreamt that I was relieving myself at the toilet and sometimes I dreamt that my friend and I were trying to put out the camp fire. After every dream like this, I woke up to find that I was wet. Then I made myself a rule. Whenever I used the toilet at any time, I made a mental note that I was doing it and then I made myself think that urinating is unpleasant and bad, any time and anywhere. The next time I had one of those dreams, all those daytime thoughts made me wake up. In no time at all, I had stopped wetting the bed altogether."

Jonathan was staring intently at Danny, taking in every word.

"Now, I advise you, don't play these games any more. Think to yourself that urinating is a very bad habit. Every time you dream anything to do with urinating, think it's bad. I am sure that it will only take a few days for you to stop. Can you promise me you'll do that?"

"Oh yes, thank you," Jonathan nodded enthusiastically, "I promise I will."

"I'm sorry Ruth, I have to go," Danny turned to me, kissing me gently on the top of my head.

As he began moving away from me, I realised that we had made no arrangement to meet again.

"Danny," I called urgently, "Are you still coming tomorrow?"

"Of course I'm coming tomorrow," Danny turned round, walking backwards, "Only if there's a war don't wait for me!"

He began running and just managed to reach a bus which was leaving the stop. The driver opened the doors to let Danny in and my last sight of him was his back as the doors closed behind him.

On my way back to the house, I again remembered that I had prepared nothing for the children to eat. I hurried and a moment later was in the kitchen contemplating a few onions and some old vegetables, which were all the food I had available. I was just thinking what miracle I could conjure up to make something out of this, when I heard my brother talking to someone outside. From inside the house it was quite normal to hear voices from the neighbouring house or of people passing by. The voice answering Jonathan sounded like Danny's, but I thought, it can't be, I saw him boarding the bus and its doors closing behind him. How much I love him! I thought, that I hear his voice everywhere.

A few seconds later a kiss was planted on the nape of my neck.

"Stop that, before I slap you." I shouted at Jonathan. without turning round.

"I will smack him too if he plays with you like that."

It was Danny.

I spun around in astonishment, alarmed to realise that he had entered the house and passed through its sorry rooms to reach the kitchen. I scanned his face to make sure that he had not changed his mind about me, but I need not have worried for there was no change in his expression, nor the slightest sign of doubt on his face to show that he might be wondering what he was doing here.

In his hand he carried several pieces of pitta bread, each filled with meat and salads.

"I nearly left you all starving and forgot to bring the kebabs," he explained.

"But I saw you getting into the bus?" I queried.

"The bus driver saw you from the window and when I told him that I had forgotten to buy you the food I promised, he stopped for me next to the kebab shop. He agreed with me that you need a little fattening."

"But you said you like skinny girls," I worried that my thinness might put him off me after all.

"You can eat all you want, my sugar dove," Danny laughed, "you'll never get fat, but you will be healthier and stronger if you eat better."

Danny put the pittas on the rickety table.

"Now I really do have to go!" he said, making his way out.

"Can I come with you?"

"It's better if you eat the food while it's still hot enough to enjoy properly," Danny insisted.

The smell was so tempting that for once he did not have to persuade me too hard to stay behind. We each took a pitta and sat all together making the most of the wonderful kebabs which tasted better than we could have imagined. Although they came from a shop quite near to our house, we never dreamed of buying them, they were so expensive. This was luxury food for rich people who did not have to consider how their money was spent. The special meal took much longer than normal as we savoured the glorious food.

We were still sitting there eating when my father entered the house. Somehow Danny had bought one too many pittas and a single one, bursting with meat and salads was still on the table. He took a square piece of meat that was resting on the top of the pitta and ate it.

"You can have it all if you want, Dad," I told him, even though I wanted my mother to have it.

"I think your mother needs it more than I do," he replied surprisingly, tumbling into his bed. He fell immediately into a drunken sleep. I covered him with a blanket and sent the children to play outside. He was obviously not as drunk as usual and would probably need some quiet.

Shortly afterwards my mother returned. I was always happy to see her, but today the exciting news I was bursting to tell added to the pleasure of greeting her. When she had caught her breath I put the spare kebab into her hand and persuaded her to come outside. There my mother sat on the stone that Danny had made special and ate her kebab. While she ate I recounted all the events of the day. I told her what Danny had told Jonathan to help him stop wetting the bed. She listened to everything I said carefully.

"It will be a miracle indeed if Danny can succeed," she said.

The next morning, the first thing I did was run over to Jonathan's bed. I was a little disappointed when I found that it was a little wet, though it was not as much as usual.

"What happened?" I asked.

"I dreamt that I went with some friends and we made a fire. Afterwards I offered to put out the fire, but as soon as I started, I managed to wake up. It just wasn't quite quick enough to catch it all, but I did do most in the toilet," Jonathan told me, proud of his effort.

"Well that's a good start, keep doing what Danny says," I said, realising that the miracle probably had to take place in instalments.

"Yes, I'm going to. You know I really like Danny," Jonathan volunteered.

There was never any trace of condescension or patronage in Danny's reaction to anything he saw in our poor home, though what he found there must often have been shocking and horrific in comparison with his own background. He never showed the slightest doubt about his relationship with me on account of my situation though I felt that he would have every reason to do so.

Danny would often surprise us with his consideration and kindness.

On the evening of our third date all the family were sitting in the house in the light of the paraffin lamp, each with his bread and jam and a cup of tea. From outside, in contrast to the chirping of the crickets, I heard a low whistle. It sounded more like a rhyming song than a whistle and I hurried outside, knowing that it was Danny's whistle, even though I had never heard it before. The tune unmistakably matched his character, it was so gentle and reassuring, like his manners.

There he stood, his presence sweetening the still evening air, holding in his hand a small wrapped parcel.

"One minute, I'm coming," I called and ran inside to say goodbye to my mother. As I kissed her, Danny appeared at the door.

"I'm sorry to barge in, but I've got something for you, something you need." He gave me the parcel he was carrying.

"May I open it?" I asked my mother.

"Of course," she nodded.

I opened the parcel with great care, my fingers pulling away the inner wrapping of white tissue to reveal a large and elegant alarm clock.

"The numbers on the dial and the hands glow so you can see them in the dark, because they are coated with luminous paint," Danny explained.

Everyone was very impressed with this most practical gift.

"Thank you, thank you," tears evoked by his unsolicited kindness welled up in my mother's eyes as she thanked him most sincerely of all, "Now I won't have to leave the house so early in the morning to avoid being late for work. I'll be able to use the extra time to help Ruth with the children."

We all joined in with profuse thanks. The clock, with its luminous hands and numbers and pretty bell alarm, we knew would provide immeasurable benefit to us, its usefulness and practicality making it more valuable than many more costly gifts.

Danny went pink with embarrassment at all the gratitude and appreciation that was being showered upon him. He appeared rooted to the spot, waiting for me to make a move.

"Well, we'd better go now," I announced finally and we left the house together.

As I remembered Danny's concern and kindness, my love for him overwhelmed me. Oh, Danny, my love! How much time have we spent apart? How much I miss you.

On the way to our destination, Danny broached the subject of his future plans.

"I know I've still got a long time to serve in the army, but I have been thinking seriously about what I should do when I'm demobbed," he explained, "I really enjoyed school and would like to be able to continue studying. I hope I can get a place at university."

He stopped walking and turned to look at me.

"What are you going to do with your education," he asked me pointedly.

My mind raced through my alternatives. I had no books to read, no one to teach me and my education until then had been far too scanty to form any practical basis for further study. I greeted Danny's question with a long, confused silence.

"I know what you're thinking, but you must still make some effort to study using any books that are available," he continued.

I wanted to tell him that I had no money to buy books, but of course, my dear Danny knew that too.

"Books don't cost anything if you go to the library. You can take a book and sit and read it there. If you don't have time to sit in the library, you can borrow the book and read it at your leisure. It still doesn't cost anything. And you can read any book, magazine or newspaper. They don't have to be brand new. If you would like, I can get them for you, but you must promise me that you will work hard on your education and not leave the books unread. You know I'm always here."

Danny cuddled me to show me that he was trying to help and not telling me what to do. I knew I would do anything for Danny and was so anxious to please this man who cared so much for me that I made the promise enthusiastically.

That evening we walked along the beach. The gentle sea breeze on our faces and the fresh tang in the air, after the stillness of my neighbourhood, imparted an unreal quality to the surroundings and created a sensation in me akin to dreaming. Danny's arm encircled my shoulders, holding me close and as we walked along, he occasionally stopped and kissed me. Some lights appeared in the distance.

"Do you want to eat?" he enquired.

"No, thank you," I replied immediately, although my stomach was empty as I had left most of my supper.

"Come on!" Danny understood and paid no heed to my answer, knowing that I was only trying to be polite.

We walked further along the beach approaching the lights, which turned out to be a restaurant, situated where the beach met the promenade, specialising in delicacies netted from the sea. Sitting on a narrow terrace outside the main restaurant, only an enormous stripy umbrella above our heads separated us from the stars. Danny ordered fresh grilled fish for us both. It looked and smelled delicious. I began to tackle my fish with my knife and fork, but hesitated when I realised that it was interlaced with bones, wondering how I could eat it. Danny came straight to my rescue, filleting out all the bones for me.

"We can't have you choking," he said, cheerfully.

Danny ordered coffee and doughnuts. The fish was not as filling as the chicken had been at our previous meal together, so I had sufficient room left this time to finish a whole doughnut.

We left the bustle of the restaurant and again wandered along the beach hand in hand. Very soon we had left all the lights behind. The beach was in pitch darkness relieved only by the light of the moon and its beautiful reflection, which resembled a million fireflies dancing over the uneven surface of the sea. White foam on the tips of the waves looked like flashes of light, here and there pricking the vast expanse of water, and the clean soft sand seemed to entreat us to sit in it, which we gladly did.

Danny put his arms around me and kissed me softly on my mouth in an embrace that lasted for a long minute. Between kisses we sat enraptured by the scene, inhaling the refreshing air and enjoying the beautiful sea that lay before us. Danny stroked my hair gently.

"Are you a virgin, Ruth?" he asked tentatively.

"What's a virgin?" I had heard the term, but never found out what it meant.

"Have you ever made love?" he explained.

But before I could even shake my head in response, "No, never mind," he added, "I can see that you are."

We lay down on the sand and he cuddled me again, pressing me close to him, causing little shivers of pleasure to chase through my body. Then he slowly stroked his hand along my leg, feeling gently further and further up the inside of my thighs, adding fuel to the excitement that knotted my stomach and the warmth that tickled a deeper part of me. I held him very tightly. I did not know where all these wonderful sensations came from or why I had never felt them before, I just knew that I never, ever wanted this evening to end.

Danny stood up and gave me his hand to help me to my feet.

"I want you Ruth. I've known other girls before you, but you are young and sweet and lovely and I want to treat you very gently. Goodness, you don't really even know how to kiss," he drew me close to him again, "I'll have to teach you."

I lifted my face towards him, but his lips only brushed mine fleetingly, "Next time", he whispered, "now I have promised to take you home."

We returned and stood silently outside my house with our arms around each other, getting ready to part.

"I'm going to make an effort to get you out of this house," he suddenly said with some feeling, "There must be a way to get you all out of this miserable place."

Little tears pricked the corners of my eyes. He cared so much.

Even more reluctantly than before, I had to separate from my love. Danny did not say that he loved me, but I felt secure with him and knew he was looking after me and that was more than enough to satisfy me.

Danny was the centre of my world from the moment of his first appearance. How my heart would ache during all those many times when Danny was away in the army. My days were spent longing for him, running at the slightest unfamiliar sound to the gap in the wall of the yard to see if he were there and leaning on the same wall, looking for him. I imagined every approaching footstep to be his and felt bitter disappointment and unwarranted anger when it transpired that the footsteps belonged to some other poor passer-by who had usurped

what should have been Danny's place in the
street.

'Danny, oh Danny, no one in the world
can match you,' my voice constricted and
squeezed, held clamped behind the lump that
stuck in my throat.

'Indeed he sounds like a truly
remarkable young man,' Josephine nodded
sympathetically, 'Did you marry him?'

'I didn't see Danny for two weeks,' I
stammered, 'I missed him badly, but he had
been away for longer periods before, so I
wasn't unduly worried. But that day, that day
…' I swallowed hard, struggling not to choke
on the words.

My brother came home clutching a
newspaper. He was crying.

"What's the matter?" I asked, greatly
concerned, for he was not in the habit of
making any outward show of his feelings. He
just sat down next to me and very gently put his
arm around my shoulder hugging me.

"I've, um, er, er, got some bad news,"
he hesitated and coughed uncomfortably, "But
I've got something good to tell you first. Danny
has arranged for us to move from this dump
soon. He persuaded the local authority to give
us a new flat."

Jonathan lost all control, racked by
intense and unrestrained sobbing. I had not seen
him cry like that since he was a little boy.

Something was terribly wrong. An icy coldness gripped me. "Jonathan, tell me. What's happened?" I gasped, panic stricken.

He handed me the newspaper. I opened it. Everything moved into slow motion. In the centre of the front page was a photograph of Danny, a black frame all round it. I could hardly see the caption.

DANNY GROSSMAN — KILLED IN ACTION. GOD REST HIS SOUL'

'No, no, dear God no,' Josephine cried out loud.

' The air squeezed itself from my lungs; I could not catch my breath. A fragment of my brain insisted that it was not true. I held the thought, nourishing it and looked again at the paper to confirm that my eyes had deceived me. But the words stood firm, pronouncing sentence. A tremendous feeling of despair insisted that the newspaper would not get something wrong that was so serious.

The room darkened and a chill emptiness engulfed me. At that moment the world stopped for me and without its normal reassuring momentum, I was falling, falling away from everything I knew and loved, sucked mercilessly into a black hole. Jonathan held me tightly but he could not hold the blackness from overwhelming me.

"Danny?" I muttered as I resurfaced, feeling a physical sickness to add to my emotional malaise. "Danny!" I called. His name will blot out the truth. But the truth reached out its long merciless fingers and clutched my fleeing reason. "Danny!" I screamed. If I shout loud enough the truth will change. "You can't be dead." A forbidding empty silence greeted my impassioned plea.

"Danny, the party! You took me to the party. On Saturday." Visions of our last meeting overwhelmed my brain. "You lifted me on to your back. Because my period pains slowed me down so. 'Please, there's no need. Put me down,' I begged you, but you wouldn't. All your energy went into carrying me home, like I was your kitbag. And oh, your lovely smell, aftershave and sweat all mixed up. I felt so sorry for you. 'Please Danny, please put me down now. You'll wear yourself out.' You said. 'It's all right, I don't feel the weight of you at all. You are as light as the feathers on my sugar dove.' You told me. That Saturday. Danny, Danny, where are you now? It can't be true, it can't be."

My mother arrived. She leaned over me, her face wreathed in tears.

"Let me die too," I pleaded with her, as if she could stop what had happened.

"Danny wouldn't want you to die and I'm certain he wouldn't want you to be so sad," she embraced me, speaking with a calm reason that belied her own emotions.

Shock stunned me preventing my feelings from the eruption that, like a rumbling volcano, was inevitable. I did not want to awaken and rise up from under its grip. I could not bare myself to the full force of my desolation, nor could I register the misery of those closest to me or the comfort they tried to give me.

"Do you want to go to the funeral?" Jonathan asked miserably.

I shut my ears to his words, but his deep sympathy released the block that had prevented me from giving lease to the most natural reaction. I wept and wept and wept, wracking breathless sobbing, out of control, desperate and hopeless.

"Why? Oh why?" I begged endlessly of my helpless, pitying mother and brother.

At last my brother's question registered. My last chance of seeing Danny was passing. I was suddenly terrified that he would be buried before I could give him one last kiss.

"Please take me there. Please take me now," I entreated my brother.

A guard stood at the gate of the camp. Behind him I could see the coffin at the back of the military parade ground covered by a plain black pall, under the shadow of a tall flagpole whose banner was flying at half mast. A large black-framed photograph of Danny stood on the coffin's lid. A solitary bugler played a mournful 'Last Post'.

I ran towards the coffin frantically shouting, "Danny! Danny!" and threw myself over it, pulling and scratching with my fingernails in a futile attempt to open it, oblivious to what was right or sensible. A sergeant major tried to reason with me, but I was unable to be rational. In the end he gave orders for the coffin to be carried to the nearest hut. The soldiers set it upon a table and opened it for me. As the lid was removed I was suddenly afraid that the sight of his damaged face and wounded body would destroy the memories of Danny that were all that were left to me.

But my fears proved groundless, for Danny lay there, hardly touched by death, looking handsome and peaceful, as if he were merely asleep. He was still wearing his uniform; the only sign of his demise was a stain of blood on his shirt, close to his heart.

I leant over the coffin to be closer to him. The same wonderful smell of Danny, mixed with his aftershave, lingered on his uniform, assaulting my nostrils, taking me fleetingly back to the night he had carried me, cementing my resolve to make him wake. I kissed his face again and again. If he knows I am here, I thought, he will realise how much I want him to wake up. My kisses made no impression.

"Wake up for me Danny. Wake up for me if you love me," I implored.

No answer. His body remained motionless, pale and cold.

"Oh God, no," I shouted, "Danny, Danny, Danny," I screamed hysterically until the exertion left me breathless and my voice grew hoarse and my throat dry. I slumped over Danny, completely drained of energy and emotion.

"Danny promised to look after us. We relied on him. He's got so much to live for," I insisted to the sergeant major and all the kind soldiers who tried in vain to comfort me, "He was always so careful. He can't be dead."

"He sacrificed himself saving the life of one of his soldiers," the sergeant major told me kindly.

That was exactly what I would have expected of my Danny. But why, oh why did he have to show his mettle under such treacherous circumstances?

Jonathan and the sergeant major gently lifted me from Danny and took me outside. The coffin was brought out of the hut and placed once again under the flag at half mast.

"We must leave it here to give all the soldiers a chance to pay their last respects and say goodbye," the sergeant major explained.

He brought a chair for me and placed it next to the coffin, allowing me to stay, even though it was not allowed, knowing that I could not be persuaded otherwise. I maintained an unyielding vigil over Danny until well after dark and would have stayed all night, if it had not been necessary finally to prepare the body for burial on the following day.

Exhausted as I was, it seemed I did not close my eyes all night, for I saw Danny sitting next to me, mostly quite upright on a chair next to the bed, but sometimes slumped sideways, nodding his head. When at last the long dark night began to recede and the light of a new day filtered into my room, my brother was sitting on the chair and all the anguish and despair I felt descended upon me again with renewed force. My brother kept me company until it was time to rise and tried to comfort me. But the comforting words were lost on me. There was nothing left that meant anything to me, and nowhere in the world I wanted to be. Not wanting life any more, my one desire was to join my Danny forever and be buried with him.

An army car arrived to convey my mother, brother and myself to the burial. Ours was the third car in the procession. The first car carried the coffin covered with the national flag, escorted by four soldiers sitting to attention on the left and another four on the right of the coffin, each holding an upright gun next to his shoulder. Danny's parents and close family rode in the second. I ached to be in the funeral car clinging to Danny but all the space was occupied by the guard of honour, who would fire the last salute.

I shivered as I stood with my family and the service took place. I felt nothing, utterly drained of emotion. The coffin was lowered slowly and deliberately into the ground. Only then did the ugly truth finally dawn on me. Danny was never going to come to see me again. At the sight of the ground swallowing him up, my apparent composure fell away.

"You've broken all your promises," I accused him loudly, "you don't love me any more!"

Shovels began tossing soft earth over him, clogging up all the passages of experience along which our love had travelled. I ran to the edge of the grave ready to hurl myself in. Hands grabbed me from all sides, preventing me from jumping, and the people who held me incurred my hatred for denying me my burial with him. Anger, frustration and torment suffocated me, standing outside the grave, just as earth and dust suffocated Danny who lay inside it.

I remained for a long time, melancholically staring at the place where my heart lay buried, every vestige of love blotted from my consciousness. All the while my mother and brother stood steadfastly by my side.

"Don't cry so! Please Ruth," Jonathan's voice broke through to me every so often, even though he was crying miserably too.

I fell onto the grave, in a final attempt to remove all the earth with my fingers. "Come back, come back!" I cried and begged him with all my soul, in the abiding hope that the strength of my tears would waken him.

Day after day I sat by the graveside, two of Danny's army friends accompanying me. Nothing mattered but to be near Danny and I could not face being anywhere else without him. Being there was my way of dying, opting out of a future alone. Without eating, without sleeping, I clung to the vile earth that had swallowed him.

"Danny, Danny come back," I sobbed and raged over and over again, my cry probing ceaselessly into the vastness of time and space, searching for an answer in the intensity of my distress, until at last, weak and delirious, I collapsed in an exhausted faint.

Looking up I saw Danny. He was standing firmly on top of the grave, smiling at me with that lovely smile I knew so well. I stared at him in disbelief, not daring to acknowledge the evidence of my eyes.

He looked straight at me.

"This isn't the way I taught you, Ruth, I taught you to survive. You must look after yourself." he said. " But this isn't the end, my love. I will come back to you, I promise."

As suddenly as he had come to me, he went. I poured every ounce of the little strength I retained into a tremendous effort to hold on to Danny, to bring him back. My love had done the impossible; it had brought him back. It should have kept him. But its power was spent. Even love is not strong enough to set back time. I have waited until now for Danny's promise to be fulfilled.

Josephine's mouth had fallen open. She nodded perceptively in final comprehension.

'So this is the boy. This is Danny,' she mumbled, almost inaudibly.

Tears streamed down my cheeks. Weak with emotional exhaustion, almost as intense as when it had first happened, I was powerless to stop them. I slumped back against my pillow sobbing helplessly.

'Ruth dear, what's the matter? You mustn't get yourself so upset,' Angela, the head nurse, wheeled the babies' cribs into the ward. She parked them between our beds and came to put her arm around me. 'What's been happening here? It seems I shouldn't have left you. Chattering is all right, but you must be careful. Your emotional state is very delicate when you've just had a baby,' she said in her kindliest manner, 'Now you'll have to try and brighten up, its time to feed your babies!'

Angela handed my Danny to Josephine and gave her baby, whom I called John, to me.

At any moment, I thought, Josephine is going to shout, 'This isn't my baby,' and pounce on me, and grab her baby from me, but the babies' fair hair and white skin dispelled the thought.

'Are my genes so weak?' I asked myself.

Josephine undid her nightgown revealing a large firm breast, which seemed capable of supplying gallons of milk, and unceremoniously gave it to Danny to suck. I was so glad that he was receiving a good feed, for my breasts were flabby and so dry that even the most diligent sucking would only produce a few drops of nourishing fluid.

'Have you noticed how alike our babies are?' Josephine remarked. Her eyes darted from Danny to John, seeming to rest longer than necessary on him.

My heart skipped a beat or two, but I retained an external calm, 'All babies look the same to me,' I answered defensively.

Josephine sat Danny upright in her lap to wind him, without bothering to support his head, allowing it to loll uncomfortably.

'Don't hold the baby like that, you'll hurt him,' I shouted at her rudely.

Quite taken aback, Josephine stared at me as if to say, 'Why are you so interested in my baby?'

I did not know how to extricate myself from this situation, but luckily I was saved by Angela.

'Ruth,' she called, reassuring me as she approached us swiftly from the other side of the ward, 'Josephine has a lot of experience you know,' she smiled at Josephine, 'Don't take any notice of my dear friend Ruth. She's become very fussy about the babies' welfare since she started helping us here. She's been a voluntary worker in the hospital for more than two years now.'

'Oh, that's why she is allowed to come and go as she pleases, unlike the rest of us,' Josephine nodded slowly, smiling, 'Do you know, I am so glad that I didn't take a private room and have had the chance to meet Ruth.'

In that moment, I hoped Josephine meant what she said and would take to me, so that we could keep in touch with one another, increasing the likelihood of my being able to see my son growing up.

'Sleep well now,' Angela bade us goodnight, 'I'm going off duty. I'll see you in the morning.' She took a last look around. 'Nurse Green, can you take the babies back to the nursery please?' she called to the night nurse who had just come on duty.

Josephine was just about to open her mouth to ask something else, when the night nurse came bustling over.

'Ladies, I'm afraid you'll have to continue your conversation in the morning,' she announced officiously, 'This isn't a private room and the lights must go out now.'

All night long I lay awake, unable to sleep because of my troubled thoughts. Had I done the best thing for Danny? Would he be better off with me who really wanted him? Should I swap the babies back again? Would I be sent to prison?

In the small hours of the morning, unable to bear the endless questions any longer, I rang the bell. After a long while, the nurse appeared.

'Nurse, could I have a pill to help me to sleep please?' I requested wearily.

'Are you sure you really need one? You know I'm not very happy about new mothers taking pills.'

'Oh please!' I pleaded, 'I've been lying here awake for hours.'

The nurse brought me one tablet with a glass of water. I found it quite difficult to swallow it, as my throat was so dry from nervous exhaustion.

It was almost ten o'clock the following morning when I awoke to find that a sign had been hung on the radio switch behind my bed.

DO NOT DISTURB — by order of the nurse in charge

I understood that the pill had taken effect, keeping me asleep until that late hour.

Josephine's bed was empty and crisply made to perfection. I thought that Josephine was probably sitting outside on the balcony warming herself in the late morning sunshine, but when I looked on the balcony, she was not here.

'Nurse!' I called frantically, 'Where's the lady who was in the bed next to mine?'

'Ruth, don't you know rich people don't stay in hospital a moment longer than necessary,' the nurse replied in a mocking tone, tinged with bitterness. 'They are all too spoilt. They've got so much money you must expect them to spend a little of it employing a private nurse at home.' A false smile crossed her face, reminding me of the expression on the face of a plastic doll.

'Didn't she leave me any message?' I asked impatiently.

'No, she wanted to wake you up, but I wouldn't let her because it would have interfered with the effect of the pill you took.'

I wanted to kill the stupid nurse, but realised that I must not make a scene. I managed to control my rage, yelling instead in frustration, 'I want my baby, I want my baby,' and began to run to the nursery.

There I found John, and Danny was gone.

'Good morning Ruth, are you all right?'

The voice made me jump. Watching John, oblivious to the rest of the world, I had not noticed Angela, who was sitting writing at the night nurse's tidy wooden desk.

'Can I have my clothes back please,' I asked, refraining from telling her that my day had begun badly, 'I can't sit around here doing nothing. I'd like to start helping out around the hospital again.'

'Well, I don't advise it,' Angela counselled kindly, 'You've done enough in the last two years. You'll be much better off making full use of the five days you have left here to have a good rest.'

Yes, she was right. I did need a rest.

CHAPTER 1

Jack and I arrived in Peacehaven four years ago, carrying one battered suitcase, which contained all our worldly goods. Starting early, we searched all day for somewhere to live, only to find that the prices were too high for us even to rent a tent. Eventually we found ourselves in Settlevale, an area that had the reputation for having the lowest priced accommodation in the city.

The buildings were old and dingy, often in a poor state of repair, haphazardly covered by sheets of metal or pieces of wood, their occupants either elderly or unemployed. Flight after flight of worn stone steps formed the main thoroughfare through the neighbourhood, which was perched on the side of a steep hill.

We made our way back to the bus, admitting defeat. Then we noticed a low, one-roomed hut, in use as a bakery, tucked inconspicuously along a side street. The dry earth surrounding the bakery was parched and cracked, as if it, like the bread, had been baked in the oven, left outside to cool, and forgotten. The delicious smell of newly baked bread wafted through the door, which stood open to allow fresh air to enter the sweltering inferno inside.

We allowed ourselves to buy a pitta each, since we had eaten nothing all day and were unable to resist the mouth-watering aroma. The baker was a short stout man, who although still fairly young was nevertheless quite bald.

'We are looking for somewhere to rent, but there doesn't seem to be much about that we can afford,' I told him, hoping that he could help.

'Well, yer in luck,' he said, 'cos I gotta place to let. The tenants jus' left. You can 'ave it if yer want.'

We asked him the cost of the accommodation.

'I gotta tell yer, I ain't gonna write no contract or nothin and I don't wanna 'ear no complaints,' he told us his terms.

'Is there anything to complain about?' I enquired.
'Nah, I don't think so, but some women are jus' too spoilt an' complain too much.'

He probably thought that I was one of those women who come from well-to-do homes and I wondered what he would have thought if he had known my real background.

I agreed to take the place under his conditions, certain that it could not be as bad as the house in which I had grown up. The money we paid constituted the entire amount of our savings. The baker gave us the key, with directions to the room and an hour to decide whether to take it.

We emerged from the stuffy atmosphere and the wonderfully cool air outside allowed some of my energy to return. I wondered what inner resource gave that man the capacity to stand next to the oven for such long periods baking his bread.

The house was approached via a small concrete platform raised three steps above the roadway, to the side of which was a wooden shed with a corrugated zinc roof. Washing, which hung from every available hook or nail, decorated the platform and a small brick built shed was located in its centre. Lengthy exposure to the elements had bent and shifted the old clay roof tiles away from their original moorings giving an impression of tidal ebb and flow, and the twisted zinc guttering was broken in so many places that it did not give any useful service at all. Luckily for us, I thought, the leaky roof need not worry us, for we had been given the key to the basement room below the platform.

Sandwiched between the platform and the giant pitch-black wall of the adjoining house was a misshapen concrete flight of steps leading down to the lower floor. The wall cast an enormous shadow over the platform, blotting out all sunlight and preventing even the merest whisper of fresh air from reaching the entrance to the room. The steps were wide enough only to allow the passage of a carry cot on wheels, making me wonder how they had found it possible to take furniture down there.

We descended the steps to the basement. Our sense of smell bore the weight of our first reaction as we opened the door, for a dank musty odour emanated from the darkness within, belying the possibility of any recent occupancy. A different, no less pungent smell issued from a cubicle that served as a toilet on the other side of the stairs. The dependence of all the occupants of the tenement on this reeking facility was plain; unlike the cellar room, it was in constant use.

My eyes alighted on an ancient brass switch. Brashly I turned on the light, feeling extremely affluent, for I had electricity. Only two items saved the room from being completely devoid of furniture. A wide mattress with mildew beginning to lace its edges occupied a corner of the floor. Some roughly folded blankets were draped across it, now little more than a patchwork of fabric pieces, since almost nothing of their original material remained. In the centre of the floor was an old fashioned luggage trunk. It looked smart and expensive at first glance, but a closer inspection revealed it to be badly made and covered with a veneer of cleverly designed plastic that hid the nails and screws of its poor manufacture from view.

The only daylight filtering into the cellar came from a 'skylight' cut into the side of the ceiling, which ran under the pavement, made of thick, translucent cubes of glass set in a square pattern in the concrete, with no facility for opening it. Every so often footsteps were heard overhead approaching the skylight grating and a shadow was momentarily thrown across the path of light reaching us, as someone in the street stepped over the 'window' above our heads.

Jack took a step backwards, his dismay and distaste obvious as his eyebrows knitted and his features formed a question mark. He said nothing, but his expression plainly told me, 'This isn't for you.' I felt only that I was being forced to carry on living the hard existence life had allotted me. I had hoped, in the way that young people do, that in moving away my luck would change.

From the day we arrived, Jack never held down a proper job, taking piecework when he could find it and spending the rest of his time drinking or sleeping. One day he came home with a guitar that has long since seen better days, and deciding that he had a talent for playing, took up a new career as a street musician.

That lunchtime, sitting on the mattress listening to Jack playing, I felt suddenly quite nauseous. I rushed to the outside toilet to be sick, but ended up only retching violently. We did not possess a fridge to keep our food fresh, or the facilities to keep it particularly clean either, so I naturally assumed that my sickness was caused by something I had eaten.

'What's the matter, love?' the old lady who lived upstairs called down to me from the balcony on the stairs.

'I feel awful and I've just been sick. I must've eaten something bad. I seem to have been off my food quite a lot lately.'

'No love, I don't think it's what you ate. When did you have your last period?'

'Period? I don't keep a record of that, but I haven't had one for a while,' I replied, wondering why she wanted to know.

'You are pregnant, my little girl. You'd better look after yourself better from now on,' she pronounced, with all the experience that old age brings.

I did not know whether to be happy or miserable. I had only married Jack because I wanted a boy so that Danny would come back to me as he had promised but I had no wish to bring a child up in that terrible cellar.

'Jack, I'm pregnant,' I told him when I returned to the cellar, 'I'm going to have a baby.'

'Hmm, er, yes, you are, are you?' Jack grunted, so disinterested that he hardly took any notice.

The guitar proved a great success, gathering a sizable profit for him in his hat, but Jack drank it all away, celebrating his new found talent.

He drank increasingly often and more heavily, on many occasions not sober enough to go to work at all. I managed as best I could to survive on the meagre amount I gleaned from his hat after he had squandered the major portion of his earnings on alcohol.

A healthy baby girl, not a boy, was born on time with no problems, signifying to me her enthusiasm to take the most that the world had to offer. Sarah was a fit and lively baby, but my one consuming problem was how to keep her warm and dry, especially since it was winter, with snow and frost covering the ground. The old luggage trunk that I had found in the cellar provided the solution. I lined it with blankets, transforming it into a comfortable and cosy place for her to sleep.

One night, unable to sleep, for hunger tugged at my empty stomach and a chill cold overwhelmed my body, I took a sleeping pill, which the old lady had given me. Sarah was asleep next to my side of the mattress in the trunk, whose lid lay open, resting against the wall.

That night my husband staggered home very late, more drunk than usual. Barely able to stand, he lurched into the room looking for somewhere to sit. He closed the lid of the trunk and sat on it.

When I woke up in the morning. I immediately sensed that something was wrong. In horror, I saw Jack's ugly drunken mass slumped over the box.

'No, no, you bastard! You bloody maniac! You drunken swine!'

As fast as I was able and with all my strength, I pushed him to the floor. The heavy thump his body made as he landed resembled the sound of my own heart. In panic I threw open the trunk. There was Sarah, not yet two months old, grey and lifeless, her mouth open as if gasping for air.

I collapsed over the edge of the box. gazing incredulously at Sarah's face, her eyes staring and sightless. Jack ran out of the room. I was so stunned that I could not even cry.

When Jack returned, two ambulance staff, a man and a woman, accompanied him. The woman lifted me from the box and sat me on the mattress. Still numb from shock, I felt no emotion.

'Take this dear,' the ambulance lady took a box of pills and gave me one with a glass of water,' It will help you feel a bit calmer.'

The man took my place, on his knees, in front of the box. After trying for some time to bring Sarah back to life, he turned his sweating face compassionately to me. 'I'm sorry, it's too late.' he said.

At that moment I wanted to shout at Jack, 'You, you murderer. You killed Sarah. It's all your fault,' but utterly defeated, I kept silent.

The man wrapped Sarah's pathetic little body in a red sheet he had brought with him and carried her from the room, explaining that a post-mortem would be performed on the body to ascertain the cause of death. Jack followed him out, his face a ghostly white.

I felt suddenly extremely relaxed and quite exhausted.

'You lie down here. You're not in a fit state to do anything now,' the kind woman lay me comfortably on the mattress and covered me with the blankets.

When I woke up, I saw Jack sitting at the table mending one of his guitar strings. I sat myself up slowly, mustering every ounce of my depleted strength.

'What happened Jack?'

Jack shot me a troubled stare, taking a long time before he spoke.

'The doctor said there's to be an inquest. Next week. He said they'll find out exactly how she died.'

His face wore a terrified expression, making me realise that there was no need for me to say anything.

I felt lost and desolate, and I was reminded how I had felt when Danny died and I had sat day in and day out feeling sorry for myself. The social worker had given me advice, in the manner that Danny often did, to go out to work. She had arranged for me to work in a big local store. There I met Jack, the store's handyman and cleaner.

The next week was the most difficult of Jack's life. He drank away all his money, bringing not a farthing home, even though in the depths of his remorse on the day of the accident, he had vowed never to touch another drop of alcohol.

The night before the inquest, Jack came back so drunk that he could not even find his own front door. A neighbour had to bring him home. It was my unpleasant task, as usual, to remove his stinking, beer-sodden clothes before allowing him to sleep on the mattress.

In the middle of the night Jack woke me up, forcing himself upon me. I tried to push him away with all my strength, but in the end gave up. He sat me up and wrenched off my nightgown, throwing my body back onto the mattress. Like a sack of potatoes, I gave him his way. After only a few brief seconds, Jack collapsed back on the mattress, leaving me struggling to sleep again all through the rest of the miserable night.

In the morning we attended the 'inquest', which turned out to be a meeting in an office with only one person, the lady coroner. We were told that the child had suffered a 'cot death', which for reasons still not known, caused the deaths of many infants. Jack was pleased with their decision and hurried away. However it seemed to me that under different conditions it would not have happened.

Through the following months I thought that I would take a job to pay the grocer, who would no longer give us credit, and the landlord, whom we had not paid since that first occasion, but with bad luck still following me, I found myself once again pregnant.

During that pregnancy I experienced no joy at the prospect of the arrival of the son, Danny, I longed for. I was consumed instead by apprehension and a dreadful fear for the baby boy's future.

Our second daughter, Judith, was born four weeks prematurely, but healthy enough for the hospital to allow me to take her home at the normal time. I returned to my sad room with more hope for her future since this time we did not have to put her in a trunk. Judith was able to sleep in a proper baby's cot, which we had been given by the kind old lady whose own children had long since grown out of it.

Now of all times, while I was striving to take care of a baby, Jack decided to disappear. In truth I was not too much upset by his disappearance since nothing useful had ever come from him and I did not expect that anything ever would. After he left, my life continued to be very hard, living in that tiny damp room.

One evening only a month and a half after Judith's birth, I went to her cot to give her a bedtime feed. Judith was an unusually placid baby who often lay quietly looking at her surroundings. Now I heard the sound of her choking, gasping for air. Quickly I picked her up. Again my baby was fighting for breath, her little face rapidly turning blue. I knelt over her on the mattress, begging, 'No, no, it can't be. Not you too!'

I slapped her, once, twice, so many times and gave her mouth-to-mouth resuscitation. Again and again I breathed into her tiny mouth trying to inflate her sunken lungs, but it was no good. Judith died having caught pneumonia from the ugly black mould that riddled the ceiling and walls of the cellar room.

CHAPTER 2

Now that Jack had left and Judith had died, I did voluntary work for the best part of two years. This was all I could do because I had no skills to offer even though people I knew complimented me on my intelligence. The voluntary work allowed me to be somewhere warm during the daytime and to keep my body going with the tea or soup I was given as I helped. The charitable work I most enjoyed was in the hospital, where I always received a hot meal and a few tips and was kept clean and warm from early morning until the evening, when at last I had to go back to my wretched room.

Of all the people who came and went while I was at the hospital, I especially noticed those women who came to have babies. I suppose that subconsciously I was envious of them, but I managed to push all my feelings right to the back of my mind, even though most of my work was involved in and around the maternity ward and particularly the nursery. The doctors and nurses gradually built up confidence in me and I was allowed freedom of movement throughout the hospital. All the staff trusted me. Some of the doctors befriended me, saying that I was capable of better things and encouraging me to improve myself. Between them they provided me with a mini-library, lending me classical literature and other high-brow books, which I found a pleasure to read and fascinating to explore. I met people from all walks of life, gaining a wealth of knowledge from their experiences and maturing in the process.

On my way back to my miserable cellar room one day, I bought a small packet of washing powder. With the little money I had available, I only bought household goods when I really needed them. As I dawdled along, like a child on her way to the dentist, my eyes fell on the inscription printed on the top of the box.

"Inside is your LUCKY NUMBER for our PRIZE winning draw."

Not being in the habit of entering competitions, I did not take too much notice. But when I opened the packet, an envelope rested on the surface of the powder with the company's address printed in the centre and the words "No stamp needed" boldly embossed across the top. Inside the envelope was a card that read:

YOUR LUCKY NUMBER
5643711
SIMPLY FILL IN YOUR NAME AND ADDRESS AND POST WITHOUT DELAY

Being so simple, I filled in the card and posted it the next day on my way to work, promptly forgetting all about it.

My routine of work at the hospital continued and I put on weight, becoming fitter and healthier than I had been for a long time, owing to the good food and warm, cheerful environment I enjoyed there.

On my arrival home a few weeks later, I found a young man waiting on my doorstep. He was beautifully dressed in a smart fashionable suit that would have made him conspicuous in a neighbourhood far better than mine. Every eye turned to look at him, a neat, clean and expensive island amongst the tumble down tenements with their junk and refuse-filled yards.

'Excuse me, lady! Am I addressing Ruth?' he asked pleasantly, as I stepped towards my door clutching my unwieldy key.

Lady! Does he mean me? But he said "Ruth".

In astonishment I dropped the key, which rattled loudly as it fell down two or three of the stone steps. The young man courteously hurried to the steps to retrieve the key for me.

Why was this man talking to me? How did he know my name?

He stood upright and gave me the key, his face flushed with blood from bending down.

'Yes, I'm Ruth,' I replied, collecting my thoughts.

'I have some good news for you,' he said cheerfully.

I opened the door, wondering what all this was about. Without waiting to be asked, the young man stepped into the room behind me, but quickly stopped short, his genial mood almost visibly shattering. Although he tried hard to continue his business with me, his concentration was lost as he scanned the room noticing the atrocious conditions in which I lived.

'Y-, you, you've won a ticket for a two week holiday abroad,' he stammered, his eyes glazed by shock, adding thoughtfully, 'We are sorry we can't give you the money instead of the holiday.'

'Ticket?' I repeated the word, creasing my forehead and gazing at him as if he were an alien from another planet. Indeed that was how he appeared to me, looking as he did and saying such strange things. I gave him a puzzled look. The astonished tone of my voice must have made him realise that I did not have any idea what he was talking about.

'You returned a lucky number in the prize draw my company organised for our washing powder promotion. Your number was indeed lucky because it has won first prize,' the young man explained earnestly, alternately transferring the file he held from one hand to the other, 'there is no money given with the ticket, but spending money for the holiday will be provided in the form of vouchers.'

By the time he had finished speaking, the reality of what he was telling me had dawned. I could not answer. My mind was in turmoil, trying to think whether the holiday would be possible for me. I just stared at him pensively, all my problems reflected in my expression.

The young man looked even more uncomfortable.

'Look, here is the ticket and my calling card,' he handed me two printed cards, one large and official looking and one small with an elaborate typeface, 'If you need to know anything or have any problems, just ask for Mark, that's me,' he smiled congenially, ' The ticket is valid at any time during the next two months. Do you have any idea when you would like to go?'

'Any time,' I was able to answer immediately, since I was not working and had no-one to look after.

'Perhaps in three weeks then, say on the 25th?' Mark suggested, taking a diary and pen from the file.

'Yes, that should be all right,' I agreed, putting all the problems temporarily to the back of my mind, but making myself a cautionary mental note that I would probably have to give him back the ticket later.

Mark made a quick note in his diary and took a step towards the door.

'Well I do hope that you enjoy it. I'll confirm this date with you before the end of the week. Goodbye.'

In a flash the door had opened and closed firmly behind him.

I barely had time to collect my thoughts when there was a gentle tapping on the door. Wondering what else the day had in store for me, I opened it and found Mark waiting to address me once more.

'I'm sorry, I forgot to tell you that you'll have to make your own way to the airport,' he told me nervously, 'the representative of the travel company will meet you there.'

Mark opened his wallet and took out several notes, which he handed to me.

'Do you want a receipt for this?' I asked, thinking that the money must be part of the holiday package.

'I much prefer a cup of coffee.'

'Of course, please do come in and sit down,' I invited him in without hesitation, determined to make amends for my oversight and bad manners and set about making the best cup of coffee I had ever made.

'Thank you for all the trouble you've taken. Are you sure you don't need a receipt?' I offered, still embarrassed by my behaviour.

'God sometimes gives receipts too,' he replied with a thin smile.

I felt secure and comfortable with this sensitive man and poured out my heart to him, telling him all about my life with Jack and my two girls in that terrible cellar.

That evening after Mark had left, I did my routine chores mechanically, giving thoughts of the holiday most of my attention, but in the cold light of the next day, I put the idea firmly back in its proper place, even with the travel arrangements taken care of, there remained too many other problems.

I made my way to the hospital, intent on carrying on my usual life. Approaching the building I met Angela, the nurse who had become a particular friend of mine. We often sat down over a meal or a cup of tea and always found plenty to chat about.

'Hello Angela, guess what happened to me yesterday!' I blurted out.

Angela was the first person I had spoken to since I had been given the ticket and I could not resist telling her the fantastic story of what had happened to me.

'That's really great! How amazing, Ruth!' Angela was very excited, much more than I was.

'Sorry Ruth, I've got to dash. I've got something important to attend to,' she apologised and hurried away like a whirlwind gathering force.

The following morning, Angela was already waiting for me at the main entrance of the hospital.

'Hi Ruth, I'm glad I've met you here. Come along with me. I've something to show you,' she greeted me with barely concealed enthusiasm, taking my arm firmly in hers and hurrying me to the staff room. There, with an air of mystery, she led me to her locker where she kept her personal things and took out a dress, which was hanging there protected by a plastic cover. 'Now I've got a reason to give you this,' she said with a flush of obvious pleasure.

For the moment I hardly knew what was happening.

'I've been waiting for your birthday or maybe a special occasion to give it to you.'

She removed the cover and I saw the last thing I had expected. The dress was one I had admired, in the window of a shop we had passed whilst out walking together one lunchtime. Angela gave me the dress to hold.

'You're going to need a few things if you are going to stay in a smart hotel, Ruth dear. Guests won't be expected to dress casually.'

Angela left me alone. Quite bemused, I put the dress on, thinking I would try it on quickly before she returned. To my delight it fitted me as if it had been made especially for me. I looked in the mirror and turned round and round.

'Even the colour flatters your complexion.'

Danny was standing behind me wearing the smile I loved so much. I knew that if I turned round the image would melt away, so I stood absolutely still, frozen to the spot, trying to keep him with me. But my eyes moistened with tears and the misty veil they drew soon dispelled the beautiful illusion.

As I was putting the dress back on its hanger, Angela returned.

'Ruth, I'm glad you are still here.'

She was carrying several plastic carrier bags. She opened them and took out the most exquisite clothes. There were two pretty blouses, a classic skirt and jacket, leather shoes, nylon stockings, pants, bras and a fluffy white dressing gown with matching slippers. Everything was new.

'These are for your holiday,' she said, her voice reflecting great delight.

I had never dreamed to own such lovely things.

'I can't possibly accept these,' I told Angela despite the almost overwhelming temptation to accept, 'Its just not fair for you to spend so much money on me.'

'Don't be silly,' she exclaimed, a cheerful grin creasing her cheeks and wrinkling her nose, 'I couldn't afford to buy these clothes myself. After I left you yesterday, I went to tell the other nurses about your ticket,' Angela explained enthusiastically, 'You are a very popular lady here you know. All the girls and the new mums have been waiting for just this chance to show how much they appreciate all the help you've given them. Even mothers who've gone home left money with me for when your birthday comes round.'

From the depths of a larger cupboard, Angela produced two perfect suitcases, complete with wheels and matching address labels. When she lifted the lid of one case, a smart camel coat, suitable for any occasion, was revealed. Angela scanned my face to gain the maximum delight from my expression as she opened the second case, which contained more clothes and shoes, some perfume and all kinds of toiletries, bought by the grateful mothers.

In a matter of minutes, I had acquired everything I would need for a stay in a five-star hotel. Thrilled beyond words, I pressed my hands together, my fingertips brushing my lips as Angela looked on, thrilled along with me.

CHAPTER 3

I rose early on the day of the journey, dressing in my smart new clothes. One of the kind nurses collected me and took me to the airport, leading me to the airline check-in desk.

'Don't forget to let Angela know the exact details of your return flight,' she reminded me before she left, 'And remember, you don't have to worry about getting home from the airport. We have all agreed that whoever isn't on duty will collect you.'

This means that I can keep the money Mark gave me, I thought gratefully.

A lady wearing a smart emerald green and navy suit met me at the check-in desk.

'I am the representative of Venture Unlimited Holidays,' she said, 'You must be Ruth. We've been expecting you. You are flying with us.'

I was most surprised that she called me by name, but she simply marked my name off on the clipboard she carried.

'Your return flight has been altered. The details are noted on this advice sheet,' she gave me the information, checked my luggage in for me and showed me where to pass through customs to the duty free area.

Angela had helped me to obtain a passport and explained what would happen at the airport, for I had never flown before in my life. But although I knew in theory what to do. I still felt confused being faced with so many people bustling about in the huge airport building. I followed some other passengers through passport control and wandered slowly into the departure lounge looking around for a phone to let Angela know about the return flight. My thoughts were wandering too, distracted by all the new things that I saw.

'You look lost!' a voice came from behind me.

I looked around and saw a tall gentleman with hair of a striking colour, who by his general appearance must have been extremely wealthy.

'Can I be of assistance?' he volunteered attentively.

'I'm just looking for a phone.' I explained.

'They are just over there,' he directed me, pointing to a group of telephones near to where I stood.

I made my call and found myself a place to sit, replacing the airline ticket in my new handbag. I looked up from my bag. There on a bench opposite me was the gentleman who had helped me. I was struck again by his outstanding hair. He had a mass of wide silver curls, which sat majestically on his head like a crown. The silver was a magnificent natural shade that had obviously been his from birth and not as a result of age. He wore an immaculate outfit fashioned from finely ribbed velvet corduroy of the palest grey. The trousers were slim, fitting him perfectly, with a slender white braid decorating the seams. The braid also decorated the matching v-neck sweater and zippered jacket, and a pale grey shirt completed the perfectly coordinated ensemble. Even his shoes paid thoughtful compliment to his clothes. A masculine face with perfect bone structure sat upon a healthy and physically fit body. Below his chin, his Adam's apple was an almost exact replica of my Danny's. Everything about his outward appearance denoted perfection.

A spontaneous smile came to my lips.

'Did you get through?' he asked.

'Thank you, yes, I did.'

'You know this is an amazing place, I always think,' he said as if the place had surprised him, 'there are so many people working here and such a large throughput of planes, yet very little ever seems to go wrong. In my experience of large organisations you need a very tight control from the top to achieve any kind of efficiency, let alone the sort that is needed to run an airport. Yet, do you realise, the airport is run on a kind of committee basis.'

'No, I didn't, but it sounds a bit like the hospital where I work. I still haven't managed to find out who's really in charge,' I smiled.

'Yes, you're right,' he nodded slowly, 'A hospital also requires efficient administration and it's important it's done well,' he leaned towards me in a conspiratorial manner, 'You work in a hospital! I should have known that you were an angel of mercy. Have you got time for a cup of coffee with me? I've always wanted to meet an angel.'

He seemed such a nice man that I did not refuse.

In the cafeteria he bought me a filter coffee and insisted that I take a cream cake too.

I'm Nelson,' he introduced himself once we were seated, offering me his hand.

'I'm Ruth.'

'What flight are you taking Ruth?'

'I'm flying to Spain on flight FT 544. My holiday's booked at the Elysee Hotel in Malaga.'

'Well, that's a coincidence. I've got a seat on exactly the same flight, only I'm afraid my trip is purely business. Have you been to Malaga before?' he asked, opening a conversation that took us from travel to transport and on to the environment and politics.

I had rarely before had the opportunity to meet such an important executive so I was surprised to find how much we had to discuss. Working in the hospital had made me much more worldly than I had realised.

'Would you like to see the runway where the planes come in to land?' Nelson offered, his eyes twinkling amiably as he spread his hand out horizontally and made a forward sweeping movement upwards with his arm. He had stimulated such a happy glow of confidence in me by then that I was probably overenthusiastic.

'Oh, yes please,' I agreed excitedly because I had never before seen aeroplanes at such close quarters and his manner convinced me that it would be well worthwhile.

We strolled to the far end of the huge departure lobby and mounted a wide stairway, which led to an enormous balcony encircling the roof. Few people had ventured onto the balcony and I wondered why. The planes stationed at the terminal entrance seemed too large and heavy ever to get off the ground, setting me thinking that was why the very biggest were called Jumbos, though who could ever imagine an elephant flying.

My thoughts carried me back to when we were children. I remembered when we found a discarded box or crate we fantasised that it was our own personal plane or bus. We sat in a line and the 'pilot' announced take off. Everyone made flying or car noises – vroom,

vroom, wheee – and someone rang an imaginary bell – ding, ding – each child in his own imaginary vehicle, until the 'pilot' announced, 'OK, we have arrived in Spain, you can leave the plane now'.

We stood leaning over the railing watching a few planes come in to land, the proof of my eyes dispelling the disbelief of my brain.

'Well, what do you think? Was it worth coming out to see?'

'Yes, well worth it,' I muttered in sheer fascination.

Just on the other side of the building I could see the runway where the other planes were taking off. Only then did I understand that the arm movement Nelson had made represented a plane taking off. I would have liked to walk around and see those planes too, but as my luck would have it the wind was strong and chilling and, like the other people, we were forced back too soon into the warmth of the building.

We walked through the shops in the duty free area. Each time we stopped it always seemed to be to look at some luxurious item. I was impressed by the vast and varied array of consumer goods for sale in the airport's splendid modern shopping complex.

'Oh, I've been looking for something like that for ages!' Nelson exclaimed, pointing at a pair of small gold discs with diamonds in the centre.

'What are they for?' I asked, puzzled by the little hinge on the back.

'Cufflinks!' he replied simply.

'But what are they for?'

'Look, cufflinks!' he turned his sleeve towards me so that I could see the cufflinks he already wore.

'I thought you had buttons there!'

'We do, but the cufflinks make an attractive decoration when the shirtsleeve shows below the sleeve of the jacket,' he explained without any trace of condescension, 'Do you mind if I buy them?'

'No, of course not.'

'Miss, I'd like these cufflinks please,' he called the saleslady over to arrange his purchase.

My attention was caught by a small camera, which had a sign next to it that read: 'Fully automatic: self-adjusting for light and distance'

'Fully automatic!' I exclaimed enthusiastically, intrigued by the idea, 'You don't need any brains.'

'Can you give me that as well?' Nelson directed the saleslady without hesitation, pointing at the camera I was admiring.

For a moment I thought that perhaps he had forgotten his camera, but we had only taken a few steps from the counter when he stopped suddenly and turned to me.

'This is for you.' He beamed from ear to ear as he presented me with the attractively wrapped package.

I flushed bright red and expelled an involuntary gasp, taken aback by his generosity. Momentarily I thought that I would dearly like to have it, but instead quickly and more than a little flustered I muttered, 'Oh no, I couldn't.'

'Don't worry,' Nelson set aside my objections kindly, 'I've always wanted to be able to buy a gift for someone that they really need. After all,' he continued, seeing that I was quite speechless, 'you will want to take some photographs to remind you of your adventure. It would be silly not to keep it. Besides, I feel so good in your company, it's worth a great deal to know that I have given you something by which to remember me,' he flattered me graciously.

'Thank you, thank you so much, you really shouldn't. It's very kind. Thank you.'

I took the camera, but held it awkwardly in my hand, far too embarrassed to place it in my bag.

Whilst still in that confused and excited state, Nelson led me to an expensive looking restaurant. Inside a large lady sat playing at a grand piano. The waiters were dressed in modish white evening suits complete with frilly shirts. lining up in a fashion that reminded me of a flock of swans, following the leader. One showed us to a table set for two, whilst another held a chair for me to sit down. The table was set perfectly, down to the last detail, complementing everything else I had seen in the restaurant.

'Would you like something to eat?' Nelson suggested.

'Oh, that would be silly, we'll be getting a meal on the plane,' I exclaimed out loud, remembering what Angela had told me, even though I must have known that we had not entered the restaurant just to admire the surroundings.

'Now I can see that you are green and have really never flown before if you think the airline meal is likely to be a satisfactory substitute for the food you'll find here,' Nelson remarked, smiling widely, 'You haven't tasted the food on the plane but there is no need, it's not for you.' He made me feel like a great lady, just as Danny had done, but as if the travel company had failed to recognise me.

A waiter brought two menus.

'What would you like, Ruth?'

'Can you choose for me please?' I asked, knowing that I could not since the menu was written entirely in French.

'Of course, is there anything you don't like?'

I shook my head.

'We'll have the *artichaut dans sauce du beurre*, followed by *bœuf bourguignon avec les petites pommes de terre nouveaux*', Nelson ordered expertly, 'We'll order dessert later'.

'Can I have it with chips please?' I added.

'Certainly madame,' the waiter nodded politely to me, not batting an eyelid.

Each course of the five-course meal was more delicious than the one before, far surpassing my previous small experience of restaurant cuisine, although the food I had eaten with Danny was a lot more satisfying. It would have been easy to linger there indefinitely absorbing the plush environment and listening to the fine music, but an announcement came over the tannoy as we finished eating, calling our flight.

An unaccustomed sense of well being so possessed me that I felt like hugging Nelson tightly, right there in the middle of the airport lounge. But I kept my impulse in check, knowing it was unseemly and would embarrass him.

The inside of the plane seemed to me confining and cramped compared with its enormous body, which I had observed from the terminal, but that in no way detracted from the first class service I received from all the air staff. Sitting next to Nelson, who had joined me in the tourist class seats, I soon became aware that my treatment was far superior to that of my fellow passengers. Perhaps the cabin staff knew Nelson well or maybe he had given them a generous tip, for I only had to raise my eyebrows for them to accommodate my slightest wish.

At first I thought that such attention was normal, but when I discovered that only I had been singled out for such excellent treatment, I felt more embarrassed than a naughty pupil sitting in the dunce's corner.

'Nelson, why are the stewardesses giving me so much attention?' I enquired uncomfortably.

'Don't worry. I fly on business all the time. The staff on this airline know me well, that's why they're looking after us,' Nelson assured me, 'Look, over there. Can you see that island? It's quite beautiful. I like to go there if ever I get a spare moment on one of my trips.'

From my seat by the window I could see each landmark that he pointed out as we passed over it. Much later I discovered how lucky we were to travel in such cloudless skies, being able to see the ground so clearly.

Quite suddenly Nelson leant towards me, putting his mouth to my ear. Feeling drunk from all the attention, I imagined that he was about to kiss me and felt that I was letting Danny down.

'Would you like to see the pilot's cabin?' he whispered.

The suggestion was most appealing.

'No, no, I couldn't,' I protested, despite the temptation, 'I've already had more than enough excitement for one day.'

Regardless of my protest, he took my hand, pulled me gently to my feet and took me straight to consult the chief stewardess.

While we waited outside the cabin, Nelson said, more than half seriously, 'There is one condition before we go into the cockpit. You must promise me that you will not like any of the good looking young men you see there.'

'No, don't be silly,' I assured him.

The pilot opened the door and led us into his cockpit.

'Hi, Nelson! I'm sorry I had to keep you waiting outside,' the pilot apologised, 'I had to hand over control and instructions to my co-pilot.'

'That's all right. What I am cross about is that you didn't come to my party.'

'Haven't you got the letter I sent you yet?' the pilot raised an eyebrow, 'I explained all about what happened there. The post gets worse by the minute.'

'OK James, I'll wait till I receive your letter before I attack you,' Nelson smiled easily.

'Well, if you are ready we can start our 'tour' with this bank of dials here,' the pilot showed us a mass of clock faces on one side of the control panel, 'I give them all nicknames,' he grinned affably, 'like the old steam engines. They had names and they seemed to have distinct faces too. When I was learning to be a pilot the names helped me remember what each one indicates. This one, for instance, is Tom. It shows the atmospheric pressure outside and was one of the original instruments to be fitted on this type of aircraft.'

The pilot went on to explain the functions of the many instruments we saw. I could not understand his explanations even though he tried not to use technical language, but it did not matter because I was enraptured by the view from the window instead.

Back in our seats, at the end of a long flight, I somehow found myself asleep on Nelson's shoulder.

We descended from the plane, passed quickly through customs and went to collect our suitcases.

'The car I ordered should be here by now. You must let me take you to your hotel,' Nelson insisted.

'I think the travel company are expecting to take me,' I demurred.

'That's no problem.'

With a brief word to the travel representative, Nelson sealed the arrangement to take me himself and we set off in a splendid chauffer driven white Mercedes.

'Ruth, would you mind if I altered my hotel arrangements and stayed at your hotel if a spare room is available?'

'No, I don't mind,' I agreed, feeling comfortable in his company and flattered that he wanted to stay there too.

It was a lovely morning. I woke early, anxious not to miss a moment of the great adventure that had just begun for me. The sun, even at that early hour, was already high in the sky, throwing its brilliant light into the room, like a spotlight illuminating the fine furniture. A colourfully woven counterpane was spread over the bed, which had been carved from dark mahogany. Behind it was a similarly carved console, housing a radio system, telephone and light fitting. In one corner stood a fine wooden cabinet of matching wood containing a large colour television. I lay among the silky folds of the vast bed like a bird floating on banks of voluminous billowy clouds.

Swinging my legs out of bed, my feet landed softly on a warm, bright rug, one of two that adorned the tiled floor. I paused only to smell the fresh flowers on the dressing table before opening the sliding door to the balcony.

The atmosphere outside was sharp and fresh, but the day was already warm. I inhaled huge gulps of salty, seaweed-scented air, leaning over the balcony to admire my first sight of the view I was to enjoy during my stay.

Where the clear blue sea met the land, a few early risers were bathing or splashing in its gentle waves, having reached it from the beach, which shone golden and clean along its margin. All around were neat, whitewashed houses and in every direction the local people could be seen beginning to attend to their daily tasks. The busyness and bustle inspired me with vitality, a joy to be alive. Keen to become part of the scene, I went inside, washed my face in the sink with elegant gold colour taps in my own private bathroom and dressed quickly.

As I descended the wide staircase to the lobby, the grandeur of the hotel impressed me greatly. In the lateness of our arrival the previous night, with my senses already overburdened by so many new experiences, I had been unable to absorb any of the hotel's opulent features. After a good night's sleep, my mind was absorbent, like blotting paper, ready to soak up anything new that I might encounter.

The lobby was huge and old fashioned, featuring a dark, solid oak desk, behind which sat members of the hotel staff, handsomely uniformed in navy and pale grey. Three elegantly framed mirrors hung on the wall opposite the desk, their position enhancing the size of the area. Vast leather sofas, the colour of ancient terracotta provided a stark contrast to the smooth and pale marble floor. In hollowed out niches, delicate stone statuettes bore a startling resemblance to several famous characters.

As I passed through the lobby on my way to breakfast, wondering at its magnificence, I met Nelson, who was waiting for me.

'Good morning Ruth, did you sleep well?'

'Yes, I did thank you. It's a very good morning. And I slept just perfectly.'

We walked through wide oak doors to the dining room, where we sat down to eat together. There was less in this room to catch my eye and my attention was diverted in conversation with Nelson, but even so I could not help but notice its size and splendour.

'Have you got any plans for today?' Nelson set his second cup of coffee down on the saucer, pushed it to one side and looked at me earnestly, as if moving the cup had given him the opportunity to see me better.

'I don't know. I'll have to ask if the travel company have made any arrangements for me.'

Nelson called over the waiter who had been extremely attentive throughout the meal.

'This young lady needs to talk to the travel representative,' he explained, 'Do you know where we can find her?' Nelson asked, giving him a generous tip.

'Thank you very much sir,' the waiter nodded his head forward slightly, 'I'll take madam to the information desk. They'll be able to help her.'

'Excuse me ma'am,' the waiter said as he conducted me to the appropriate desk, 'but did you know that the hotel offers a sauna and massage studio, as well as the outdoor pool and tennis courts, for the benefit of its guests? And we can arrange almost any service you may require from laundry to tailoring. I'm sure you've already become acquainted with the hairdresser and other shops behind the foyer.'

'Oh no, I didn't know,' I replied, wondering what other services they could possibly provide.

The clerk at the information desk looked through a sheaf of mimeographed papers.

'Well madam, the travel company haven't made you any tour arrangements as such,' he looked up at me, 'but your travel vouchers may be used to pay for any of the tours which operate from this hotel. I have some details here if you would like to look at them. Of course you are free to do as you please, like the other guests.'

He gave me some leaflets and I returned to the lobby where Nelson was waiting.

'I think I'll take one of these organised tours, ' I said, showing him the leaflets.

'No, don't do that. I've got some free time today and it will give me great pleasure if you will let me show you around.'

Nelson's manner, as before, was persuasive and after the experience of the previous day, I was glad that he had asked me.

'Thank you, I'd like that very much.'

'With your permission I'll release my chauffeur. What I want to show you is much better visited on foot.'

'Of course, you know best,' I agreed.

The chauffeur, who had been waiting in attendance, was grateful for the break.

'Thank you Mr Rubin, sir. Thank you madam. I hope you have a very nice morning.'

We set out at a leisurely pace, stopping to look in several craft and antique shops on the way. I was fascinated by the many beautiful objects displayed for sale everywhere, concluding that the area was an exclusive part of town. We walked along wide avenues generously planted with different kinds of palm trees and featuring small tropical gardens ablaze with colourful flowers, which allowed the passer-by to rest in a shady tranquil setting.

Nelson knew the resort so well that although we seemed to be wandering without plan, he was in fact gently leading me to the town's central square. On one side stood an impressive stone building set on three floors, which displayed many windows glinting in the sunlight. The façade was highly decorated in the fashion of an era when craftsmen had great skill and plenty of time to spend on their art.

'This is the town hall,' Nelson told me, 'It was built about two hundred years ago by a local nobleman as a country home for his beloved wife. She was very sickly and couldn't stay with her husband at the royal court because it was vital for her health that she took the sea air, which was good for her. Look at all those balconies!'

Nelson drew my attention to row upon row of balconies, each awash with masses of flowers in large window boxes. 'All the rooms on the sea side of the building have balconies. The lady couldn't walk far, you see, but those balconies enabled her to indulge her love of watching the sea, outside in the fresh air.'

I looked closely and noticed that every balcony had its own unique architectural feature.

'When the lady died,' Nelson continued, 'her husband couldn't bear to keep the house, with all its associations, so he sold it to a local landowner. It passed from hand to hand until no one could afford to keep it any more. By then a town had grown up around it and the government took it over for its own use.'

In front of the building was a large bronze statue of a stately man.

'This is one of the first mayors of the town,' Nelson informed me.

I looked at the base of the statue to see if anything was written there. Nelson saw me looking.

'It's funny isn't it? No inscription! The mayor was well-loved and respected, that's why they erected a statue of him, but they didn't put anything about him on it, not even his name.'

'How do you know so much? How do you know this was the first mayor?' I asked in wonder.

'Whenever I visit a place on business I make a point of discovering as much as possible of the local history,' Nelson smiled widely, 'I've always been interested in history, especially that of other countries. And most places, even if they're quite small, have a tourist office. They are usually more than willing to tell you any local anecdotes.'

We began walking back slowly, passing a pink and white ice cream parlour, which displayed every colour of ice cream imaginable.

'Come on, let's get an ice cream,' Nelson took me to the counter, 'which do you like?'

I hesitated, examining the huge variety of exotic flavours.

'There are so many. I don't know what to choose.'

'Well, if you'll let me advise you, I've found that banana, with continental chocolate and orange sorbet make a perfect combination.'

'Three kinds! Oh, I'll never be able to manage three,' I exclaimed, putting my hand over my stomach as though I already felt replete.

'Yes, you will, they're not so filling and the sorbet is all water anyway.'

The ice cream looked so irresistible that I was grateful Nelson wanted to persuade me.

Three large scoops of ice cream were piled on top of my cone, which was scarcely big enough to hold one. We left the parlour, sauntering along in the direction of the hotel. I managed to balance my cornet quite well for some way until it suddenly toppled to the ground.

'Oh no, oh dear,' I sucked in my breath in embarrassment. We had gone too far to return for a replacement.

'Have some of mine,' Nelson urged me instead, with such persuasiveness that I could not even consider refusal. This gave me a chance to sample yet another wonderful flavour. His close proximity to me sent little shivers scurrying between my shoulder blades and all the way down my back.

The weather was hot, but pleasantly so. The light cotton dress which Angela had given me contributed greatly to my comfort since it was sleeveless and open, but covered just enough of my shoulders to prevent sunburn.

We returned to the hotel in time for lunch.

'I'll just see if there are any messages for me,' Nelson said, as we passed the reception desk.

The receptionist took a folded slip of paper from one of the wooden pigeon holes that held the room keys and gave it to Nelson.

'Oh, I am sorry Ruth,' he apologised, looking crestfallen after examining the paper, 'It seems something urgent has cropped up. Something I just can't put off. I had hoped to have lunch with you, but now I'll have to go,' he said in a hurry.

'It's OK,' I replied cheerfully, 'I've had a lovely morning.'

I felt lost in that grand dining room on my own and quite lonely, having already become accustomed to Nelson's genial company, but made the best of the afternoon on the beach, lazily basking in the bright sunshine.

My heart quickened when I encountered Nelson just before dinner in the grand lobby, for I had hoped that we would meet, although we had not made any arrangement.

'I am pleased you are here Ruth. I was beginning to think I'd missed you.' he greeted me with a relieved sigh, as though he had spent days searching for me, 'Would you like a drink from the bar?'

We sank into comfortable easy chairs, he with a good whisky and I with plain fruit juice. I had never had the opportunity to learn to appreciate anything else and was nervous to try anything stronger.

'I'm sorry that you had to spend lunchtime alone. May I give you this little token in the hope that you will forgive me?' he said, pulling a little cream coloured box from the jacket pocket of his exquisite hand sewn evening suit and giving it to me.

I took it and lifted the lid. Inside, on a black velvet cushion lay a beautiful cameo brooch. Quite stunned I put my hand over my mouth and bit my lip, knowing that I could not accept this gift and yet not knowing how to refuse it.

'Don't even think of refusing,' Nelson instructed firmly, seeing my dilemma, 'It will make me very happy if you will accept it. I want you to know how glad I am to have met you here,' he said with obvious sincerity.

A thrill of happiness engulfed me. I could hardly believe that so worldly a gentleman would pay me such a compliment.

'Thank you Nelson. It's really beautiful,' I spoke warmly, a happy glow in my cheeks, 'I am very glad to have met you too. I wouldn't have found my way around so well or enjoyed myself so much without your excellent guidance and good company.'

After dinner, Nelson invited me to sample the local nightlife. We found an uncrowded nightclub advertising cabaret only, luckily for me, as I did not know how to dance. Nelson ordered cocktails and we settled down to watch a traditional programme of song and dance, performed by a six-person troupe. The men, in sober peasant costume paid court to ladies whose swirling embroidered skirts reminded me of a kaleidoscope. We sat out of doors in the soft moonlight, the strong perfume of flowers wafting over us, carried gently by a warm breeze. In this perfect setting, all my senses alive in such wonderful company. I wondered how I came to be part of such a paradise.

Nelson made me feel intelligent, he valued my opinions and always treated me like a lady. For the next two weeks we spent our time together enjoying every imaginable pastime and pleasure that the holiday had to offer. I learnt a great deal about local history and customs, visiting many interesting and beautiful spots under Nelson's expert guidance. Every sporting activity provided at the resort was made available for me to try. Time just flew away on a heady cloud of sightseeing, culture and romance.

One day a hot and powerful wind was blowing strongly enough to carry with it any small loose items that it found in its path. Pieces of paper floated this way and that, changing direction as often as a dithery old lady changes her mind. Nelson and I were forced to return from the beach before everything we had taken there with us was blown away. Back in the hotel room, we found that sand had accumulated in all our clothing.

'Ooh, there's sand everywhere and it's really scratchy,' I remarked, shaking myself in an effort to get rid of it.

'Here, let me help you,' very carefully Nelson helped me remove my blouse so that the sand would not irritate my skin any more.

As he lifted the blouse away, I felt Nelson's warm breath on my neck and his arms encircling me in an affectionate embrace, his lips imparting little kisses on my neck and shoulders. My shoulders arched upwards to meet his kisses, and my body was ready for him to comfort and love me. The sensation was so pleasurable that I let him lay me on the bed. Bit by bit areas of Nelson's skin became exposed and caressed similar areas of my skin, first his arms, his chest and then his legs and torso.

The scratchy sand took me back to a windy evening I spent with Danny.

Dust swirled thickly all around us, so that we might have been in the middle of a desert storm. Danny picked me up and began running with me. He gently tossed me on to a heap of coarse building sand that stood nearby. In an ecstatic abandoned mood as we lay on the sand kissing, Danny undressed me until I had nothing left on and the wind rushed all around my naked body, together with its sandy companion, slapping and stinging me. Danny fell on top of me and somehow his clothes too were completely removed, drawn off by the magic pull of the wind. Slithering and sliding, we made love on the cascading particles, which pricked our skin like a host of flying needles. The sand was both underneath us and dancing on the wind, ticklish and painful at the same time.

"Ow, oh, ow," I giggled, feeling the pain, but not minding, it was such fun.

"It's Cupid," Danny laughed, "He's aiming all his little arrows at us, just us!"

We stayed there for a long time, savouring the exhilaration of the moment, our involvement with one another and shared bliss sheltering us from the wild elements, cuddling each other and making love again.

Nelson gently slid his leg from my body pulling the sheet with him. 'You are so beautiful,' Nelson interrupted my reverie.

'Oh, Nelson,' I blushed, pulling the sheet right up to my neck, feeling that I had betrayed Danny.

'I'm going to find another concert to take you to,' he changed the subject, feeling my discomfort, 'You are such an intelligent listener, it's a pleasure to be your companion and I know you really enjoy going.'

Almost before I noticed or could prepare for it, the day for my return arrived. In chaperoning me, Nelson had gradually neglected his business, so he had to stay behind to complete it. Nevertheless, my contentment and lightness of spirit spilled over into the flight home, making me feel as if I were still on holiday. Even when one of the kind nurses collected me and took me back to the hospital, I was so absorbed in recounting my wonderful experiences that my real life continued to elude me.

I returned to my voluntary work, happy and satisfied with life. But every evening as I made my way back to my awful room, the thought of it filled me with a sickening sensation and when I arrived I was enveloped by blind misery and a dreadful chilling fear.

Then suddenly I started being sick again. I am pregnant! I thought and felt an overwhelming desire to have the baby, sensing that this time it would be Danny.

Working at the hospital, I made every effort to maintain my valued status, since I knew that in my condition no other job was available to me. A week before the baby was due, I entered hospital and was given the best bed, in the maternity ward that I knew so well. When the time came for my confinement, I gave birth to the boy I had wanted for so long.

CHAPTER 4

The key was a bad fit in the stiff lock of the cellar door. I fumbled with it for a few moments, just as I had done since I arrived on that first day with my husband Jack.

Baby John was crying. In the distance I could hear the sounds of car doors slamming.

'They are coming to arrest me,' the thought agitated me. I held my breath, waiting for the frantic thudding of running feet. As quickly as possible I shut myself inside expecting to hear impatient knocking on my door or the insistent thump of somebody trying to enter by force, but I was alone with John.

The cellar was dark and the stain of dripping green-black mould, which clung to its northerly wall, was now bigger and blacker than ever. The powerful smell of fungus permeated the air. In the middle of the floor, the dilapidated mattress still lay where I had left it, the blanket draped across it appearing now brilliantly colourful, like a mid-day rainbow, in contrast to the dark tones that dominated the rest of the cellar.

A churning hopelessly pumped my stomach and the only thought that calmed it was the fact that I had escaped having to bring my Danny to this dump. Resignedly, I laid baby John down on the mattress.

'John, you just lie here quietly for a moment, I'm going to clear the room and move your cot as far away from that damp wall as I can.'

This I did, not because of any special feelings for the baby, but because I considered that I must discharge my responsibility fairly towards him. I picked my way across the room until I reached the cot, which was made from strong wood, once painted white but now yellow and worn with age. One of its slatted sides could be pulled down for easy access and there were even two different positions for the mattress. Looking at it again, I recalled that more hopeful time when I had considered it a delight, whenever I had adjusted the side to lift Judith out, to have the use of such a luxury. I put John to bed and I too was glad for the blessed escape of sleep, drawing a temporary curtain between me and my miserable existence, which bore no hope of improvement.

In the dawn of a new morning, I rose determined to shake off the dark gloom that threatened to envelope me. A gentle tapping on my door reawakened my nervous fears.

'They've come for me!' flashed through my mind, but I quickly dismissed the thought, feeling that I had heard that knock before, a long time ago.

'Come in,' I called, still tense, for my neighbour rarely knocked.

No-one entered. At last I trudged across the room and gingerly opened the door. There before me stood Mark, the same kind young man who had given me the ticket almost a year before.

'I haven't entered any competitions this time,' I breathed out, my shoulders sinking in amusement and relief.

A gentle smile travelled up to Mark's eyes, showing the recognition of a shared experience.

'I was passing this way to give someone who lives nearby his winning prize and I remembered what good coffee you make. I just couldn't resist knocking on your door,' he explained.

'Do come in. Please excuse the state of the room,' I ushered him in gladly.

Mark followed me into the room but seeing John, he halted suddenly.

'Oh, I'm sorry,' he exclaimed, 'I'm disturbing you. I didn't realise that your husband has returned.'

Looking embarrassed, he headed straight for the door.

'No, it's not like that,' I forestalled him, 'Jack hasn't been back since the day he abandoned me. Sit down please. I'll make you that coffee and tell you how I came to have this baby.'

I pulled forward a rickety chair, making it as comfortable as I could for him and brought the coffee. I sat myself on the mattress next to Mark, the only person who had ever visited this room and I told him all about how Angela and my friends at the hospital had made it possible for me to take the holiday and about my meeting and friendship with Nelson on the holiday, culminating in the birth of the son I had longed for.

At the mention of the baby, Mark's face took on a serious and sad expression. He levered himself to his feet, walking slowly towards John, who was beginning to whimper in hunger.

'He's a lovely baby. Can I hold him for a moment?'

'Yes, of course.'

With a bound, I reached the cot first, lifted John and gave him to Mark. John lay peacefully in Mark's arms despite his hunger.

'What's his name?' Mark enquired, carefully returning John to me to feed.

'John,' I said simply.

Mark's attention wandered round the room and his eyes rested momentarily on the huge black spot on the wall.

'I really must go,' he said suddenly, 'I'll see you again soon, I'm certain.' Mark pulled open the creaky door and left.

CHAPTER 5

I was woken up by John coughing. The thought that he, too, had caught pneumonia passed through my mind, and I felt like his executioner. I picked him up. While I was changing him there was a thunderous knocking on my door. The urgent banging insisted that this was not a social call. My whole body arrested in frozen attention as an icy terror gripped me.

'That's it, John. They're coming to take you. And me, they'll put me in prison until I rot.'

Quickly I put John in the cot and covered him. As I finished, the door opened.

'Are you Ruth?'

Two massive uniformed women stood framed in the doorway. Their identical blue suits gathered in a wide black belt and hair pulled back flat and shiny in a tiny bun made them look like prison warders.

'Can we come in?' the taller of the two asked.

'Her question sounded to me like a threat. I could not speak, for my tongue was stuck to the roof of my mouth.

The tall woman marched over to John's cot, picked him up and began to undress him. In that moment I felt the earth shake beneath my feet and with all my remaining strength. I prayed. In my imagination I saw prison bars, cameras flashing as I arrived at the courthouse, my friends, the kind nurses, giving evidence against me, Angela particularly, accusing me of ingratitude.

The second woman took a large instrument from a leather pouch, which hung heavily around her neck. It looked like a transistor radio with two rigid nails protruding from its casing, like antennae from the head of a snail. She strode across the room and stabbed the nails into the skin of each wall in turn. A high-pitched whine, like a burglar alarm issued from the machine as the nails made contact with the wall and a small lever, part of a dial located in the top panel, jumped over a black marker, each time registering a number in the red section of the dial. As the numbers registered, the woman ominously jotted them down on an official form that she had on a clipboard in her hand.

The tall woman finished undressing John, took a stethoscope from a large holdall, fitted it firmly into her ears and listened to John's chest. I just stood here, feeling as if a snake's poison were oozing through my blood, waiting for them to handcuff me.

After what seemed like a very long time, the second woman finished probing the walls and turned to me knitting her brow severely. She looked me straight in the eye, 'This child can not stay here,' she said sharply.

At that moment I wanted to shout, 'I only did it to save my child's life. I've had two daughters die here. Please, please understand me,' but I had no opportunity to speak, for the woman continued, 'A few days ago, an educated and well-spoken young gentleman came into our office and told us, 'I pay taxes to enable you to take care of people who need help.' He asked us to visit this address and save a child who is living in a hovel. Now, I can see from my instruments that he was quite right to bring you to our attention. Not only will your baby ...'

When she said the words 'your baby', my mouth fell wide open and my ears started humming so loudly that I could not hear her voice. The woman's intimidating demeanour had put everything out of my mind except the fear of being caught. Slowly my battered senses returned to this world. I felt like throwing my arms around her and embracing her.

'We will be placing you in a temporary apartment immediately, until we can find you more permanent accommodation,' she finished.

I could hardly believe what was happening. Bitter remorse gripped me for having exchanged the babies. My brain buzzed with questions. Why, oh why did I give my Danny away if everything was going to be all right? Can I tell the truth and they'll help me find my Danny and forgive me? Will I ever see him again? But only one of my questions was answered as I remembered a saying that my mother had been told when she complained about an unwanted pregnancy.

'When a baby is born, his luck is born with him.'

It seemed that this baby possessed good luck and I was sharing it with him.

I dressed John snugly in Judith's all in one suit and began gathering the more suitable of Judith's clothes and some of mine.

'I'm sorry, Ruth, but we can't allow you to take anything with you from here,' the woman stopped me.

I thought about the dress Angela had bought me and my other 'holiday' clothes.

'Oh, but what will I wear? I must take my clothes with me,' I demurred, quickly folding my favourite dress.

'Well, I suppose your clothes won't be a problem, but you mustn't take any clothes for the child, or any linen or blankets. Those will be provided by our department.'

The social workers took me by car to a temporary apartment in a pleasant area of the city. It was in no way luxurious, but its simple warmth and cleanliness made it seem like a palace after the smell and damp that I had borne all my life.

The flat was filled with solid old-fashioned furniture. A telephone stood on a bookcase in the spacious living room, which doubled up as a bedroom with a convertible 'put you up' settee and a cot in the corner for John. There was a simple kitchen and, from my point of view, the most luxurious feature, our own spotless bathroom.

'You should be comfortable and warm here, until we find you something more permanent,' the tall woman pronounced, showing me how to work the heating. 'The young man also told us that you have been helping voluntarily in the local hospital.'

'Yes, that's right,' I confirmed, slightly puzzled.

'Well, we contacted them to ask if they would give you paid employment. They are so impressed with you that they told us they'd be glad to any time. If you like, we can make arrangements for you to start next week.'

'But the baby?'

'You won't have to worry about him, my dear,' smiled the second woman pleasantly, showing the first sign of human feelings since I'd met her, 'One of the student nurses who is taking special training in child care will look after your baby until a proper arrangement can be made.'

When the social workers had left, I went to investigate the bathroom. Steaming hot water spurted from the adjustable shower head into the gleaming white sink, allowing me to wash my hair without any fuss or difficulty, as I had only been able to do before on my wonderful holiday. I felt as if I were once again residing in a first class hotel.

During the next few days, I gradually settled into my splendid new environment, constantly marvelling at my good fortune. Promptly, as arranged on the fifth morning after my move, a pleasant young girl arrived to take care of John, and I was ready to begin my new job at the hospital.

While I waited outside the administrative office for the hospital's secretary to arrive, many old friends approached me, glad to see me and wanting to know how I was. Among them was Angela, who halted in her tracks when she saw me.

'Oh Ruth, now I know why you never let me come to your flat,' she accused me vehemently, 'Why on earth didn't you tell me? Why did I have to find out from that social worker how you've suffered?'

'I'm sorry Angela, I couldn't. The memories were too painful. I just wanted to leave them in the past where they wouldn't hurt me any more.'

'But Ruth, if you'd given me the opportunity I would have helped you. I knew you weren't well off, but never imagined you lived in such terrible conditions. No-one should have to live the way you did. We would never have sent you back there with John. How could we have sent you back?'

I was helpless in the face of her scolding and my bewilderment showed. Angela's attitude swiftly softened. Her voice choked with emotion and she clasped my hands warmly in hers.

'I'm so sorry Ruth. It should never have happened. All I can say is that, thank goodness, from what I understand, things will be better from now on. I only beg you not to keep things from me any more,' she said with a sympathetic smile.

At that moment a smart, rather fussy woman arrived. 'I am the hospital secretary,' she informed me.

I said a hurried goodbye to Angela and promised to meet her later. The secretary took me into her office and helped me fill in some official hospital employment forms, registering for work. When they were complete, she stood up, straightening her skirt and patting her immaculately arranged hair.

'I understand that you are very meticulous about your work. We need someone who will work carefully, to clean in the X-ray department and in the other areas of the hospital where we keep our diagnostic apparatus and other sensitive machines. You will be responsible to Mrs Stone, who's in charge of cleaning. I'll leave you with her and she'll explain your duties.'

The secretary led me to a small office where we found a grey haired lady who was introduced to me as Mrs Stone.

'You know where to find me if you need me,' the secretary told me formally and she was gone, her feet tapping in precise even steps as she disappeared down the corridor.

I loved my work, particularly at the times when I could see the machines working, and watch in fascination the marvellous tasks they performed. When they were not in use, or the staff operating them took their lunch breaks, I would delight in carefully dusting and polishing them, and sometimes even replacing parts that the staff had neglected to return to their correct places.

I was very careful not to dislodge any parts and took particular notice of the position or arrangement of anything moveable. On one occasion, the department was thrown into a minor panic because a loose wire was impairing the function of one machine. A roomful of patients waited, and the specialist technician would not be available for a couple of hours. While the nurses ran hither and thither, like leaves in a storm, trying to rearrange the schedule and a doctor complained to the administration office on the telephone, I began my own quiet investigation. Within a few minutes I had gently relocated the familiar wire in its correct place, invoking the immense gratitude and awe of the whole department. After that I gained sufficient confidence to pay more attention to the instruments and would often stay overtime to put them in perfect order ready for the next day.

My part-time employment was not particularly well paid by most people's standards, but to me, who was used to managing on next to nothing, it earned just enough for me to buy essential clothing and other things that I needed.

One afternoon after work, on a shopping excursion, whilst wandering around the children's department of a large store, I heard a familiar voice.

'Hello Ruth! Do you remember me?'

A young man appeared from between two large rails of clothing. I pursed my lips in puzzlement, trying to remember where I had seen him before.

'It's me, Mark, the one who brought you the ticket!' he said, approaching me.

'Oh hello!' I greeted him with gusto, 'I can't thank you enough for sending me those social workers.'

'Well, I'm sorry I did,' he smiled enigmatically.

I threw him a questioning glance, surprised by his response.

'When you moved, I didn't know where you had gone,' he explained, 'I couldn't contact you, or find out what had happened to you and I was embarrassed to go back to the social workers.'

'Oh, never mind, you've found me now and thanks to your concern I can offer you a cup of coffee in a much nicer place now,' I said gratefully.

Mark bent to his knees and put his little finger into John's hand. 'Hello John,' he said, wriggling his finger playfully, 'do you like shopping with Mummy? He's grown, hasn't he?' Mark stood up, beaming at me.

I nodded in happy assent, but my Danny broke into my thoughts, making me resent John being in his place.

'Can I join you and help with your shopping?' Mark requested pleasantly.

'It's not important. I don't have to do it now,' I said shyly, wheeling the pushchair towards the heavy plate glass door of the shop. Mark leaped forward before me and held the door open for us to pass through, as Nelson had done so often for me on the holiday.

'Please will you allow me to treat you, this time, to a nice cup of coffee and a cake,' he ventured, pointing to a small coffee bar opposite the store.

'Are you sure? With John?' I asked awkwardly.

'Yes, of course! He can sit on my lap.'

Inside the café, we took a seat near the window. Mark lifted John from the pushchair and sat him on his knee.

'They do a lovely chocolate cake here,' Mark commented, 'You must try it. I must say it is fattening, but you don't have to worry about that.'

The cake Mark ordered was indeed wonderful. Morsels melted in my mouth in tiny bursts of flavour, like raindrops splashing in a puddle. Mark made sure that John too had a chance to sample it, for he fed him tiny bite-sized pieces from his own plate.

'Ruth,' he turned to me, 'It's my birthday in a couple of days time. I'm giving a small party. Can I ask you to join us?'

I took a quick shallow breath and looked at him, one eyebrow slightly raised. My mind filled with the impracticability of accepting. The student nurse only came during the daytime, leaving me with no-one to baby-sit in the evenings and at weekends. As I opened my mouth to voice this difficulty, Mark spoke as if he had been reading my mind, just like my soldier Danny had done.

'My sister has a baby too,' he assured me, 'She's not married. In fact she never was married. She lives with all of us in my parent's house. I'm sure another baby won't make any difference for one evening.'

A party conjured up scenes of merriment and fun such as I had rarely experienced. I wanted so much to go, to break the monotony of my lonely existence.

'I think you'd better check with your sister first and then phone me and let me know,' I answered despite myself.

'Yes, I'll do that,' he agreed.

Mark beamed broadly and widened his eyes in delight at the opportunity of obtaining my phone number.

Later that evening when I had released the nursery nurse, the telephone buzzed.

'Hello, Ruth!' Mark's genial voice sounded through the wires, 'I've spoken to my sister and it's OK. She said she'd be very pleased to meet you. In fact she said you have a lot in common to talk about.'

Until that moment I had hardly dared to even think about going to the party. Now it was going to be possible, little butterflies tickled in my stomach as my excitement grew. Even as Mark spoke, making arrangements to collect me on Friday evening, I began thinking about which of my holiday outfits I would wear.

The next day, as usual, I went to work. I searched out Angela during my lunch break.

'Angela, guess what? I've been invited to a party!' I told her without stopping even to greet her properly in my enthusiasm, 'The nice young man who arranged my holiday has asked me.'

'Oh Ruth, how exciting! I'll baby-sit for you, of course,' she offered without a moment's hesitation, 'You must go to the party,' she insisted, 'In fact, I wanted to offer to baby-sit before, but I didn't because I thought you might be upset if you knew you had a babysitter and nowhere to go.'

'Thank you ever so much, Angela, but you don't have to worry. I'm taking John with me. It's all been arranged.'

'The offer is open if you need it, Ruth, but the important thing now is that nothing stops you going to the party.'

CHAPTER 6

I laid John in his carrycot and carried it to the back seat of the minicab, settling myself next to him. An uninterrupted ten-minute drive brought us to the outskirts of the city, where we reached an almost hidden turning off the main road. The driver had to bring the cab to a standstill in order to negotiate the narrow entrance.

As we swung in, it seemed that we were driving through an arch carved out of a tropical forest, for the greenery on either side of the entrance had knitted together, forming a leafy tunnel which encompassed the car. Inside the tunnel we had to execute a difficult zigzag manoeuvre to bring us to a narrow tarmac-laid path, where a sign fixed on a low branch proclaimed 'Private Road'. 'It's so narrow here, how will the cab ever be able to turn around and go back to the main road', I asked myself.

Immaculately maintained houses nestled on either side of the lane, their white walls gleaming and their red roofs smoothly polished. But this was their only similarity, for each was unique in character, designed and built with the craftsmanship, which is the hallmark of a master builder. Beside each house stood a small garage, built in a style that exactly matched the house. A well-tended garden in the shape of a half moon completed the approach to every house. On the edge of one garden, a statue beckoned to an invisible companion, and in another, an elaborate and shiny brass sundial waited patiently under artificial light to begin its true work when the new sun arose.

At the end of the road we found a minute circular island, no bigger than a double bed, enclosed by a low raised brick wall and filled with unkempt shrubs with variegated or oddly shaped foliage, the like of which I had never seen before. It took two attempts before the driver could position the car precisely enough to steer around this awkward obstacle. Finally we faced the most beautiful house in the road.

This mansion was hidden from its neighbours by an enormous garden, laid with a neatly manicured lawn. Fruit trees planted here and there scarred the lawn's perfection. A brightly illuminated private tennis court stood at the back of the garden.

As the car stopped in front of the house, Mark appeared at the door. Finding myself in the centre of a setting I had so little expected quite unnerved me. I felt out of place and wondered what people would think of Mark when they saw a woman of my background, with a child, coming to visit him. I was so overcome by embarrassment that I decided to tell him that I was going home, but just then an attractive young girl opened the door of the car.

'Hello Ruth! I'm Mark's sister,' she smiled affably, 'I'm so glad you are here. I've been waiting for you.' She greeted me with great warmth, as though she had known me for years. 'This must be John. Can I take him for you?'

I nodded, my self-consciousness beginning to evaporate in response to her reassuring manner. She lifted John from his carrycot and rubbed noses with him playfully.

'Come in with me Ruth, I'll show you where he can stay.'

I felt a lot easier knowing that she had a baby too, for everyone at the party would think that I was her friend and accept me. In truth I only wanted to listen to the cheerful music and drink a little wine to make me merry.

'The babies will be better off upstairs, where the noise and the smoke won't affect them,' Mark's sister explained, leading me straight up to the top floor. We entered a nursery such as I had never imagined might exist. Its tiny occupant wanted for nothing, his complete comfort carefully planned, right down to the cartoon characters who performed on the pattern on the curtains, ensuring a stimulating environment. In a high chair sat a baby.

'This is Gary, my son,' Mark's sister said, 'Oh and by the way, I am Vicky.'

'Vicky,' I sighed, 'He's beautiful! In all my time at the hospital with all the mums and their children, I never saw such a beautiful baby.'

Gary's huge pale eyes were surrounded by long curly eyelashes. A dimple dented each cheek, deepening further when he smiled, a smile that brightened his already rosy complexion. His wide little nose was shapely but defied description and a mass of golden curls was his final crowning feature. John was a very ordinary baby by comparison with his podgy face and two prominent rabbit-like front teeth. For just a minute I wanted to know how my Danny looked.

'This is Nanny,' Vicky introduced a lady in a blue uniform who had just entered the room. And we must go down to join the party now. It's already started,' Vicky's voice broke into my thoughts. She pulled me gently towards the stairs down to the party room.

'Ooo, it's so loud!' my hands flew involuntarily to cover my ears.

The noise of the discotheque was quite deafening to me, unaccustomed as I was to party music. The reception room was full of smoke. Standing prominently on one side was a solid oak bar, its finely sculpted frame shiny from years of lavish polishing. Opposite, a wall of books had been opened cleverly in the centre to reveal the discotheque, normally concealed behind doors that gave the impression of being part of the bookcase. A sumptuous green velvet sofa had been pushed against a wall, leaving oceans of space in the enormous room for dancing. Small groups of guests stood chatting and sipping bubbly drinks, while others sat watching the handful of dancers who had been enticed to join in the rhythmic drumbeat and flashing lights in the centre of the floor.

'What will you have to drink, Ruth?' Mark enquired, approaching me and indicating the comfortable sofa for me to sit on.

'A glass of sweet sherry would be very nice,' I replied proudly, I knew what to ask for, remembering the drink I had grown to like on my holiday.

Mark hurried off in the direction of the bar.

'Are you Ruth?' a young man came over and made himself comfortable on the sofa next to me. He too was handsome, like the baby, and dressed in the very latest fashion down to the finest detail including an ostentatious watch that graced his wrist. 'I've been told all about you,' he continued, making a few casual remarks to draw me into conversation. He spoke in a haughty tone that indicated to me that he was the son of a wealthy family.

'Here you are Ruth,' Mark returned with my drink, his face breaking into a perplexed smile when he saw the young man, 'This is Prince,' he introduced, sitting down next to me on the opposite side from Prince.

I had no chance even to sip from the glass. Prince seized my hand and whisked me onto the dance floor. He was a master of the art of charming the girl with whom he danced. Fluent in all the steps, he moved effortlessly with the music as if creating a work of art. Under an irresistible magnetism, I felt impelled to join him in the rhythmic movement. Mark behaved with perfect politeness as the host and did not interfere with Prince, allowing him to dance with me several times.

When the party was in full swing, Prince brought me a long cool drink, which I took to be orange juice.

'Ruth, do try this. It's very refreshing,' he persuaded.

'Oh yes, thank you,' I accepted it gladly. I had already consumed five small glasses of sherry and was certain that this golden liquid, which had a brightly coloured stirrer poking through the ice that bobbed on its surface and a slice of orange adorning its edge, would dilute my intake of alcohol.

I was making the most of the cool drink, sipping it slowly when Vicky purposefully sought my company, taking a vacant seat next to me. We were soon deep in conversation.

'Do you know why I didn't want to marry my baby's father?' Vicky confided with a sigh, 'It's because he wanted to marry me only because I was pregnant.'

'Is that what he told you?' I asked incredulously.

'What he actually said was even worse. "If you're pregnant, I'll marry you!"'

'Goodness, I wouldn't have married him either,' I agreed with her readily, thinking to myself that if my life had the advantages she enjoyed, I would not want to get married anyway.

'Do your parents know who the father is?' I enquired.

Vicky shook her head firmly from side to side indicating that they did not.

'Ruth, have you finished your drink?' Prince interrupted, pulling me to my feet.

My glass was now three-quarters empty. I deposited it on the table and he escorted me to the dance floor. The tempo of the music slowed and the lights dimmed, creating a romantic mood.

'My parents are on holiday in the Bahamas at the moment,' Prince began telling me about himself, 'My father has left me his 1949 Buick convertible to use when I like. I've brought it with me tonight, instead of my Ferrari. I'll take you for a ride in it later if you agree. My father is an appeal court judge, you know and that's how I came to meet Mark. His father is a judge in the High Court too. We met at a party at my father's legal club. Of course, I mostly mix with the families of the legal fraternity. I do have a lot of influence, you know and my friends respect that.'

Prince pulled me very close. The warmth of his body and the smell of his aftershave overwhelmed my senses. He began gently stroking my back, his fingers moving steadily downwards, spreading a thrill with them that permeated my whole body.

'What's happening to me? I feel so light headed.'

'There's nothing to worry about,' Prince leered at me, 'The lights won't go on again for a long time. I've arranged for the DJ to play a long slow record so I can dance with you without being disturbed.'

He brushed his moist lips over my ear lobes and planted light sensuous kisses on my neck. Deftly his hands worked above the material of my blouse to release the fastening of my bra. My breasts suddenly tingled with sensation, released from the confining pressure of their elastic restraint. A warm ticklish feeling that I had not felt for a long time rose from deep inside me.

We danced together as one being. I felt my skirt being lifted, in the middle of the room with all the other guests around us. But for me it had ceased to matter. An irresistible desire for him engulfed me. I lost all control of myself and did not care who would see me or what the consequences might be. I only wanted him to be naked with me.

The lights abruptly snapped on, blazing impulsively, and everything stopped.

'You bastard!'

All eyes turned in our direction. Mark prized us apart and punched Prince in the face, knocking him over. Confused, I stood stock still, trying to understand what was happening. Mark seized the collar of Prince's jacket and hauled him to his feet, ready to deal him another blow.

'That's enough Mark,' Vicky intervened.

'You are scum,' Mark exploded, 'They told me what you did. I've warned you enough times, you spoilt idiot, not to do that. Leave this house,' he shouted furiously at Prince, 'and don't ever come back here again. If you don't do as I say right now, I'll have to tell your father all about your behaviour and the nasty tricks you play.'

'Mark, I murmured, 'I want Prince very much.'

'I'm sorry Ruth, I'm sure that's what you think, but at the moment you don't know what you want. Prince put a drug in your drink to make you want him,' Mark declared.

I did not understand what Mark meant, but had no opportunity to ask him to elucidate, for Vicky guided me tenaciously away to the top floor.

CHAPTER 7

Bright slivers of light pricked my eyelids. Slowly I lifted them and much faster shut them again. Yet in an instant they opened again, wide with wonder.

Femininity and elegance pervaded every corner of my surroundings. A modern, ivory-coloured dressing table, fitted wardrobes and bookcase were all of Scandinavian design, oozing with style through their plain and practical lines and contours. A sofa for two near the window seat was covered with a pretty pink and gold flower print fabric, whose theme was repeated in the curtains and bedspread and appeared in miniature on the lampshades and tiny frilled cushions that lay scattered on the bed and window seat.

Near where I lay, a specially designed unit accommodated a portable television, a record player comprising the latest technology and a collection of some one hundred long playing records. It was a young woman's paradise, her every whim considered.

I slipped hastily out of bed, intent on finding my clothes, but succeeded only in locating my blouse and slip. There was no sign of my skirt, but draped carefully across the dressing table stool was a long, gossamer-thin silk dressing gown.

Should I touch it? I felt quite unworthy, but my outfit was incomplete. There was no choice but to wear it.

I started to leave the room wanting to find the nursery, when my eye caught a glimpse of my reflection in an intricately carved antique cheval mirror, which stood on ornamental black legs, its frame of gold-painted leaf work glinting in the morning sunshine. From a room, identical to the one in which I stood, beyond the gold foliation, stared a woman who faintly resembled me. But this person came from the stone age, where she had never needed to comb her hair, nor had the opportunity to look in a mirror. Large dark rings encircled her eyes and her tongue when I poked mine out, was yellow and felt sticky.

I looked around for a brush or comb. The dressing table revealed nothing suitable, prompting me to approach the nearest door and open it. There to my astonishment was revealed an exquisite bathroom, decorated in a delicate mixture of pink and grey shades. The room was warm and inviting.

The pale grey of the porcelain bathroom suite, which included a bidet, was picked out in the design on the pastel hand painted tiles and in the monogram 'V' sewn into the fluffy pink towels. A ceiling high mirror covered the wall by the bath and two pale grey cabinets hung artistically above a double vanity unit like a pair of doves flying in to roost. The unit displayed the articles I needed to make myself presentable.

When I was tidy enough to be seen, I crept out into the wide hallway, with no idea where I was going or where to look. Eight or nine doors confronted me. Fortunately, one that stood open was the children's playroom, where I found Vicky feeding John, and the beautiful baby sitting on a cosy rug on the floor, propped up by pillows.

'Oh Vicky, you should be feeding Gary!'

Vicky flashed me a vivacious smile. 'Are you up already Ruth? I didn't think we'd see you until this afternoon, after what happened last night.'

'Oh heavens,' I jumped nervously, 'I'm supposed to be at work.'

'Now I see that I was right. You aren't awake yet,' Vicky laughed, 'It's the weekend. You don't have to go to work today.'

'Oh, of course!' I cried, remembering, 'Shall I take John now?'

'It's all right. I've almost finished.'

'Do you know where my skirt is?' I enquired.

'When we brought you to my room last night, you were sick all over it,' Vicky recounted, 'It was all the alcohol you drank and that trick of Prince's that made you sick.'

I had no idea to what she was referring and looked at her in puzzlement.

'I mean the pills he put into your orange juice,' Vicky elucidated, but seeing that I still looked blank she continued, 'You know, Prince. He's such a spoilt brat ....'

'Yes, I didn't like him at all,' I broke in, 'He was a pain in the neck.'

'What!' Vicky stared at me with wide eyes, 'I am surprised to hear you say that. You very nearly slept with him.'

'Me?' I turned scarlet with shock and embarrassment. Only now did I realise how strong the drink was that he had given me.

'Your skirt will be ready after breakfast,' Vicky changed the subject, diplomatically ignoring my confusion.

'I can't go down like this,' I protested, fingering Vicky's dressing gown, 'Oh, I'm sorry, I had to put it on.'

'It's all right Ruth, we don't stand on ceremony here. You don't have to dress for breakfast. I'm not.'

It was true. Vicky also wore a dressing gown, even more casual than mine, for it was mini length. This made me feel more comfortable, although I would still have preferred to wear my own clothes.

'Nanny!' Vicky called.

The ample woman I had seen the night before appeared smiling in the doorway.

'Oh Nanny, here you are! I've fed Gary and John. Will you be able to keep an eye on them please, while we go and have breakfast?'

At the top of the staircase we encountered Mark. Across his outstretched arms lay my skirt, laundered and precisely pressed.

'Oh thank you Mark,' I enthused gratefully as he gave me the skirt. 'Please will you excuse me,' I glanced at Vicky, 'I'd like to change straight away.'

'Yes, of course. I'll go down and fix breakfast,' Vicky announced, bounding down the wide stairway, three steps at a time.

'I'll wait here for you,' Mark declared cheerfully.

'I am sorry about yesterday,' I said quietly, lowering my eyes, 'I feel so guilty that you had to fight with your best friend.'

'You needn't worry about that,' Mark retorted, 'I've been looking for an excuse to give him a punch or two for a long time. I have to thank you for giving me a reason. In fact, I'm hoping to find another opportunity.'

I smiled at him, relieved that after all I had not abused his hospitality.

A few minutes later, wearing my own clothes and feeling much more relaxed, I rejoined Mark and together we descended the stairs to the breakfast room. Vicky was standing in front of the cooker frying a few large sausages. The sight of the oily sausages and the smell of the hot fat sent my head spinning and made me want to run from the room.

'I'm sorry,' Vicky apologised, noticing my expression and the greenish hue of my face, 'I forgot that you're not likely to appreciate anything fried this morning.'

'I can only face a glass of grapefruit juice,' I murmured.

'Of course! You'll find a jug of grapefruit juice and one of orange juice on the table outside. Mark squeezed them specially for you.'

Vicky directed me to sit on the patio in the fresh air, while she and Mark ate their fried breakfast with a hearty appetite. I drank my fruit juice slowly, gazing from my vantage point at the magnificent garden, with its brilliant green tennis court and glittering swimming pool, which sprawled invitingly before me.

I recalled the words of the rich lady, 'Do people really live like that?' only now it was I asking the question. The freshness of the day and peace of the garden began to revive my befuddled brain.

'Has your hangover gone? Mark joined me, leaving Vicky to do the washing up.

'Yes, thank you Mark. I do feel much better now. It's very quiet here.'

'My parents went out last night, so that we could have the house to ourselves for the party. I don't expect my mother to be up before lunchtime, they came home so late. But my poor father had to go out early,' Mark's forehead furrowed slightly, 'He's sitting on a case this morning.'

'On a case?' I queried.

'Yes, my father is a judge,' Mark explained casually, 'and we will have to behave with the utmost propriety so as to give the newspapers no excuse to write about us,' he added with a humorous twinkle in his eyes.

It occurred to me to ask why his sister had an illegitimate baby if his father was such an important man of the law, but I did not possess the courage.

Early in the evening, Mark took me to a smart restaurant for dinner. Apart from a few occasions on my holiday with Nelson, I had no previous experience of the kind of exclusive establishment in which we ate. I enjoyed the meal tremendously as I briefly relived that happy interlude.

We returned to Mark's house to collect John, whom Vicky had been looking after. He was scrubbed and clean in his nightwear and positively blooming with a bright healthy smile.

'Thank you very much for minding him for me Vicky. You've taken care of him so well.'

'It was a pleasure to have another baby to keep Gary company. I'm going to interfere in your life more often from now on,' Vicky commented mischievously, 'But you won't let that put you off will you? You will come here again, won't you Ruthie?'

'Yes, of course,' I replied, knowing that I could never visit here again, because of my background, even though I wanted very much to return.

'Take care Ruth,' Mark waved affectionately, after paying the minicab driver.

It was not until I reached my small apartment and was alone once again with John that I realised how much I had enjoyed being at Mark's house. A little past his usual bedtime, John had fallen fast asleep. As I laid him in his cot, the telephone rang.

'Hi Ruthie,' Mark's voice sounded on the line, 'I just phoned to make sure you arrived home safely.'

'Mark, it's only a fifteen-minute drive,' I answered, feeling flattered.

'Yes, I know. I wanted to know that you got home all right and to wish you goodnight.'

'Good night Mark. Thanks for calling.'

I replaced the receiver with a

wonderful feeling that for the first time in my life since Danny's death, someone was concerned about me.

CHAPTER 8

A complex job kept me occupied the next morning whilst I eagerly waited for lunchtime to see Angela.

'Do tell me Ruth, how was the party?' she asked immediately.

'I could write a book about what happened to me in the last day and a half,' I disclosed dramatically.

'Don't write a book, tell me!'

I recounted the whole adventure to her, concluding with the last telephone call I had received from Mark. From time to time Angela punctuated my story with interested questions concerning the house or the guests' outfits, but made no comment at all about Mark, probably because she, like me, thought that a person of my status in life would not be welcomed by a judge.

At home, later that day, the telephone rang again.

'Ruth, can I come to see you please?' Mark asked purposefully.

'Me?' I queried, wondering whether to encourage him.

'Yes, of course! Can I?'

'All right!'

'Thanks, that's great! I'll be there in just about an hour.'

I bathed John and gave him a light supper before his bedtime. I thought about my own Danny as I busied myself looking after John's needs. I knew that if he had been with me, I would not even have considered leaving him in the care of a stranger. But in some ways I was glad that my Danny was not with me, for I was able to leave John without any misgivings and concentrate all my efforts on my job. Deep in my heart, I believed that John's luck was following me.

Mark arrived. As before, he was genuinely pleased to see John, picking him up and cuddling him.

'I thought we'd go to a restaurant for dinner,' he suggested tentatively, looking at me over the top of John's head.

'I'm sorry, I won't be able to go out tonight. There's no-one for me to leave John with, but if you're hungry I can make us something,' I ventured.

'That sounds nice, but are you sure you want to go to all that trouble, Ruth?'

'Nonsense, it's the least I can do. I'll leave you two together whilst I get the food ready.'

John giggled merrily as Mark bounced him in the air, made funny faces and played peek-a-boo with him, gaining as much pleasure as John did. Soon John, quite exhausted, fell fast asleep in Mark's arms.

The meal was just ready. I put John to bed and invited Mark to the table, where I served the meatballs I had prepared.

'This is amazing,' Mark commented in surprise, 'How did you manage to prepare meatballs so quickly?'

I looked at Mark with a mysterious smile and kept my secret for a while longer. On my days off I usually did a quantity of cooking and stored the food in the freezer until I needed it. After Mark add eaten and enjoyed the meal I told him my trick.

Mark ate my food! I never imagined that he would touch it, lacking freshness as it did from its long sojourn in the freezer. Yet he showed no trace of being spoilt and left nothing on his plate. He probably doesn't want to embarrass me, I thought. Nevertheless, his thoughtfulness was just like Danny's and it sparked in me an inner glow of sympathy and contentment. I wanted to hug him, but the moment slipped past. Mark insisted on clearing the table and helping with the washing up.

'Shall we sit down and relax now?' he asked, when the kitchen was tidy once more.

I smiled in assent and led the way in, pausing for a moment beside my small record collection to select a favourite LP of instrumental music, which I placed deftly on the turntable.

'Do you realise, Ruth, that the whole evening of the party, I didn't have one dance with you?'

Before I could reply, Mark answered for me.

'It's all right. I know Prince didn't leave you any opportunity.'

I nodded slowly with a frown of regret. Mark's marvellous knack of reading my thoughts precisely had not failed him.

'Come Ruth, dance with me now.'

I glided into his arms, happy to make amends for the disappointment of the party. We danced, closely and quietly as John slept and we were alone.

'I've forgotten the pills for your drink,' Mark quipped light-heartedly, 'so I can have your all to myself!'

'You don't need pills to make me want to dance with you.' My voice was calm but firm. I wanted Mark to be in no doubt. 'Prince only used that trick because no girl would stay with him for more than a few minutes,' I continued, 'He had to do it to have any chance.'

'Mmmm,' Mark disregarded my small outburst and nudged me slowly around some more. How very gentle he was, so gentle and comfortable that I nestled closer to him, resting my head against his strong chest.

'How secure I feel with you,' I murmured, 'like a little girl with her big brother.'

Mark stopped dancing and held me firmly, looking intently into my eyes.

'I don't want you to feel like my sister. I am in love with you.'

I took a deep breath. Multitudinous thoughts raced along the nerve wires of my mind. He's only talking. He can't have thought things through seriously. He's got carried away. He hasn't really realised who I am.

'Don't think that I haven't thoughts about the fact that you have a baby and aren't married. I know it could cause problems with my family, especially with my father.'

Then I knew that he has thought quite clearly before he spoke.

'Please Mark, don't be silly! Don't mess up your life for me. You could easily find yourself a respectable educated innocent girl and start your life afresh. You don't need a poor second hand woman like me.'

Mark said nothing more; in reply he only drew me closer. My body temperature rose sharply as he stroked and teased my thick black locks.

Hesitantly I asked, 'Have you been with any girls?'

Mark did not look at me now, his head bent snugly into the hollow beside my own.

'I have had plenty of girls,' he replied, 'but I've never felt the way I've felt for you, from the first moment I saw you.'

'Oh Mark, how can you say that. I can't understand,' I disentangled myself from him so that I could look into his eyes, 'I am poor and lost in the world.'

'Love isn't motivated by money or position,' Mark broke in, 'From the day I brought you the ticket, I've thought only of you.'

He caressed me as Danny had done before, causing a tingly excitement to transcend the pleasant fluttering that I felt at first and I knew that I wanted him very much.

'You know, making love is a wonderful experience when a man and woman love one another,' Danny had told me.

Do I love Mark? I asked myself.

It was in an old vineyard that I lost my virginity. The vines grew adjacent to each other in long straight rows, each plant trained along an open latticed fence that supported it. These rows stood evenly spaced, one next to another, hundreds of them high above the fence. The tops of their growing shoots and leaves met and intertwined forming a lacy green ceiling. Bunches of plump, juicy grapes resembling clusters of exotic pearls, hung along the length of these leafy galleries.

"No one will ever see us here!" Danny exclaimed.

He took me by the hand and led me to the beginning of one of the tunnels that ran between each row of plants. The ground was covered with fine soft grass, the kind that often grows in sunless locations. We had to bend down to enter the "tunnel" which was like entering a huge pipe. Our eyes took a little while to adjust to the dimness, for in contrast to the sunny road outside, only an occasional pencil thin shaft of daylight filtered through between the vines from the bright sky above. All around us were bunches of grapes.

"They aren't ripe yet," Danny remarked.

He took off his jacket, put it onto the ground and laid me gently upon it. There was only room between the two rows of plants for one person lying flat and another lying sideways. Danny lay sideways and with the most tender kisses his lips brushed my mouth and throat. Slowly he began unbuttoning my blouse. Even though the weather was hot and it was very warm in our arbour, I started to shiver.

"Why am I shivering," I asked.

"Don't be afraid," Danny said.

"I'm not afraid. I don't know what to be afraid of!"

Danny looked into my eyes tenderly. He finished undoing my blouse and let it slip easily away so that it fell to the side of my body. I felt his lips all over me and at the same time absorbed his wonderful smell tinged with aftershave. I did not want him to stop, even to draw breath.

"I love you," he whispered passionately. It was the first time he had ever said those words so clearly to me and I delighted in hearing them.

Now Mark and Danny merged into one person. Danny slipped his hand underneath my bra and loosened it. Gently he caressed and squeezed my nipples. The trembling subsided as warm and exciting sensations arose within me. I wanted him very much. He traced his hand under my skirt but made no attempt to loosen it.

I looked into his kind face and honest eyes and knew that he respected me and would never use me.

He carefully lifted my skirt and laid it over my tummy. Slowly and gently he pulled my underwear away, until they lost their contact with me, all the while planting warm kisses from my throat to my belly, causing my excitement to deepen. Loosening the rest of his clothing, he coaxed me to move my body into the position that he thought would be most comfortable for me. Shyly and quietly I did exactly as he wished. He lay down over me, supporting his weight on his arms and kissed me fervently on my eyelids, on the tip of my nose and firmly on my mouth. I was still engulfed in the fever of his wonderful kisses as I felt his body slowly coming into contact with mine and a strength and power in the closeness that made me want to melt and mingle with his whole being. His fingers intimately stroked the source of my desire.

Mark drew me into a comforting hug and kissed me affectionately. I lay there, feeling the physical warmth and vitality of his body upon mine and I felt even more strongly the warmth and love of his heart.

'You are ready for me. I can feel it,' he said earnestly.

Inside me I yearned for the consummation of his presence. Momentarily he stood, divesting himself of his own clothing. I raised my arms to accept his warmth, which caressed and enveloped me. Fires raged and swelled within me, striving to climb the mountain following the wild stream, in an ecstasy of sensuality forgotten since the time when I loved Danny and he was mine. Mark's gentleness, the consideration he continually showed to me, the fact that he cared for me, whoever I was, entirely won my affection, causing me finally to reach the pinnacle of passion, subsiding to a completeness, a full state of womanliness that I had not imagined. True to his character, Mark only allowed himself release on the moist skin of my belly.

'Now is not the time for you to have another baby,' he observed, 'not until my son John has grown a lot more, and not anyway until I marry you.'

There was nothing I could say and so I kept silent.

CHAPTER 9

The shrill jangle of the telephone pierced the dusky peacefulness of the night, jolting us rudely awake from a luxuriously comfortable position asleep in another's arms. So very snugly did we fit together that I could not help wondering why I had never found it possible to sleep restfully next to Jack, my wayward husband. Lying with him, any position had been awkward. Some part of him was either digging irritatingly into me or cutting off my circulation, until I reached the point where his clumsiness was so disagreeable that I longed to throw him away from me. Even with Nelson I had been unable entirely to relax, and with Danny there had never been any place to relax. Mark and I linked together easily as if we were interlocking stitches knitted into a handmade fabric.

Mark gently disentangled himself, sprang to the telephone and brought it to me.

'Hello, is Mark there?' the cultured feminine voice seemed clipped and anxious.

I beckoned to Mark with raised eyebrows and a nod, and held out the receiver to him. He stood listening for a few moments.

'I'm really sorry Mum, I should have realised that you would worry. It was selfish of me not to let you know I'd be late,' Mark's brow furrowed, genuinely contrite, 'Look, will it be all right if I come home in the morning?'

The room was so quiet I could faintly hear her voice. Why is it, I wondered, that some people are blessed with parents who take an interest in their welfare and care for them when they are grown up and long past an age when that kind of involvement is even expected? Mark is older than me, yet his parents still show him affection, concern and worry.

'Yes, yes, I know,' Mark's practical tone interrupted my thoughts, 'Yes, bye.'

In the depths of the night, with sleep banished, my contemplative mood was slow to evaporate. I stared into space, a faraway expression haunting my features. Mark sat earnestly beside me.

'In my family, even after we children are married, my parents hope that we will let them know our plans,' Mark explained, 'For instance, if I were to go away for the weekend, or perhaps even for the day, if it were something special. They want to be involved, to maintain an interest in our lives.'

He put his arms round my waist, lifting me back onto the open sofa and planting a full rosy kiss on my mouth.

'Mark,' I murmured amorously when he paused for breath, 'I've got work in the morning. Goodness knows what the time is. I think we should get some rest now.'

'I'm sorry,' he whispered, relaxing his arms, 'But give me one last kiss.' His eyes narrowed saucily and his nose wrinkled persuasively in an expression of affectionate jesting. He squeezed me firmly, taking my lips briefly but with passion, all his fervour concertinaed into a few short seconds.

Deliciously, the events of the night replayed themselves as I slowly regained the wakefulness of the dawn. I opened my eyes expecting Mark to be next to me. All I found was a crumpled empty hollow in the blankets.

'Mark! Mark, where are you?' I called, hoping he was in the bathroom.

Silence gathered, together with disappointment in the absence of a reply. Opposite the sofa bed stood a heavy folding hospital screen on wheels, which had been salvaged when the Hospital Friendly Association replaced this old fashioned screen with modern ceiling to floor gliding curtains. To make the screen more attractive, I had replaced the original faded and torn blue cloth covering with a bright floral material, whose brilliant colours both divided and enlivened the room. Behind it was John's cot.

I slid my feet from the settee onto the bedside rug, stepping quickly from the rug's warmth across cold pale green linoleum until I reached the cot. John lay still sound asleep. Tucked firmly between the mattress and the bars I found a large folded paper, with my name on it. Eagerly I unfolded it.

My Darling Ruthie Breakfast is ready. There are also a few sandwiches to take to work for your lunch. Bon appétit
Lots of love
Mark

XXXXX

PS Left early to have enough time to change before work.

The lump in my throat was only released after I allowed a few tears to fall onto my cheek. I hurried to the bathroom, stopping myself from peeking into the kitchen first, wanting to save my breakfast treat for later. Someone was singing loudly and joyfully, like a liberated canary. The song matched my mood entirely, happiness and contentment bubbling over for all the world to hear.

Who is singing?

It's me, taking myself by surprise, doing something I had not done for a long time, singing heartily from sheer delight.

I reached for the tap to fill the bath, relishing a soak in masses of soapy bubbles. The outside door abruptly opened and banged shut. "Is it Mark?" I thought. "Has he forgotten something? Oh, of course, it's Ellen, the trainee nursery nurse for John. Goodness is it that late?" No time for a bath. My hand turned the shower lever instead.

A few minutes later, dressed and hurrying more than I had meant, I sat at the kitchen table hastily consuming the tasty breakfast Mark had prepared for me. There was no time even to get John up. I dashed for the bus, leaving Ellen in charge.

CHAPTER 10

In a tiny cubby hole between the X-ray room and the huge office housing the hospital records, I had appropriated a small space to keep the few articles I needed for my work; a shelf with a neat collection of dusters, polish, solvent and brushes. By mid-morning I needed some clean dusters and was searching industriously in the cupboard.

'Ah, it is Ruth, I assume!' A deep voice boomed warmly in the space behind me.

'Yes, that's me,' I turned around. A pleasant smiling face greeted me. The large man behind the face and the voice seemed to fill the corridor with his genial presence. There was a shiny bald patch on the top of his head and what little hair that remained was almost completely grey. He wore an immaculate office suit of the kind favoured by the hospital administrators. In one hand he carried a finely finished gold-initialled black leather briefcase.

'I am Silvester Kleinman,' he leaned forward and shook my hand vigorously.

'Oh, er, yes, Mr Kleinman,' I flushed slightly in bewilderment, unable to imagine why a hospital official would want to see me. But although he must be important, he was not in the least intimidating.

'I work for the company who manufacture and supply most of the sensitive technical equipment used in this hospital,' he explained.

'What kind of equipment?' my eyebrows knitted quizzically.

'All those delicate machines that you work with, my dear. You know, the X-ray apparatus, the incubators in the special care unit and so on.'

'Oh yes, of course,' I nodded vigorously, hoping I had not sounded too ignorant.

'I've been receiving excellent reports about you, Ruth. I hope you don't mind me calling you Ruth?' he declared animatedly.

I smiled faintly.

'I've been told that you take very great care of our machines, that you take pride in them and tend them with respect. Once, I've been told, you even solved a technical difficulty because you knew the exact location of the wiring.' The briefcase was pulling his body into a lopsided attitude. He moved it to the other hand. 'My company is extremely pleased with the care taken of our equipment here in this hospital. All credit is due to you.'

'I think they are remarkable machines,' I bubbled, 'and I feel it is an absolute duty to wash your hands before touching them.'

'I think I quite agree with you.' Mr Kleinman's jovial face beamed a wide smile. He shifted his briefcase again. 'Shall we go into the head nurse's office?' he offered, 'It will be more comfortable than the corridor.'

'Oh yes, of course,' I agreed hastily. Curiosity made me want to hear more of what he had to say. He led the way into the partitioned half glass sanctuary that constituted Angela's niche in the main office. Mr Kleinman motioned for me to sit down and opened his briefcase on the compact desk.

'Do you mind if I smoke?' he enquired politely.

'I think you'll be in a lot of trouble with the head nurse if you do.' I smiled, remembering some of the bold statements Angela made about smoking and the smell it left behind.

'Well in that case, I'll get straight to the point. You must be wondering what this is all about. As I told you, I work for the hospital equipment manufacturer that supplies this hospital. The board of directors have sent me expressly to offer you an important post with our company. The position will involve visiting all the hospitals to which we supply our machines and apparatus, and teaching their staff the best way of looking after them, using the methods you have used so efficiently here. Then from time to time you will return to each hospital to make sure that everything is running smoothly. You will liase with our engineers and if you feel that anything technical needs attention you will have the authority to ask them to look at it. And of course you will have a new company car permanently at your disposal.'

I listened carefully while he spoke, almost disbelieving him, almost certain that he really meant to speak to another Ruth. It could not be me. Could it? Because of John? Could the 'luck of a baby' change a person's whole life?

Mr Kleinman appeared not to notice my pensive stare.

'Your salary,' he continued, 'will probably be considerably more than you earn here.' He quoted a figure that was at least five times my present wage.

That's it. Mark sent this man. Like the social workers he sent. But no, it doesn't feel right. There's too much Mark doesn't know about.

Mr Kleinman continued explaining. My thoughts might be wandering, but I still looked attentive. I focussed my attention back on Mr Kleinman.

'Of course, we don't expect you to take on all this responsibility without any training,' he said, unclasping his hands from the tidy position they had assumed on the desk in front of him, lifting them upwards for a moment in a gesture that reminded me of a benediction and re-clasping them firmly again. 'We will be sending you to join a short course of a few weeks duration, to help you gain the essential technical expertise you will need initially. Then later on there will be further courses to keep you up to date with the most recent developments.'

'Oh dear, I'm afraid I've got a baby – John,' I faltered, my voice rising in pitch, for a moment feeling unusually close to John and caring tremendously for his welfare, 'and I can't leave him in the evenings.'

'Please don't worry about that my dear,' Mr Kleinman smiled reassuringly, 'the course will occupy the same hours as the job itself, which, by the way, are the same as you work here. And the study centre in Company Headquarters isn't far from where you live,' he paused, 'Is there anything else worrying you?' he asked, noticing my expression.

'Mr Kleinman, I'm sorry, but I can't drive,' I said, realising what else he had said that was bothering me.

'I didn't think that you could. No need to worry about that either. We will make provision for you to take lessons and you will have time to learn to drive.' He reached into his briefcase and took out some papers. 'Now, do you want to ask anything else?'

'No, you seem to have told me everything, thank you,' I said, hoping that I sounded more positive.

'Well I'm sure all this is a lot for you to consider,' he added kindly, 'I expect you'd like some time to think about it?'

'No, I don't need any time. It's just what I want to do. When do you want me to start?' I wanted to settle the matter before he could change his mind.

'That's lovely Ruth. In that case all that remains for me is to fill in this form with you.' He waved an ordinary sheet of typed paper. It had space at the bottom only for my name, address and signature. 'And you can start the course the week after next. Now you can use the time until then to organise whatever you need. And above all, do arrange some driving lessons and take your test as soon as possible. When you have your licence, you can collect your car directly from the garage.'

The form filling took only a few moments.

'Angela tells me that a week's salary in advance will be of some use to you,' he handed me an envelope with a cheque for a sum of money such that I had never seen before nor handled in all my life. 'Ruth, I'm sure we'll meet again soon.'

Mr Kleinman rose to his feet, proffering his hand in another vigorous handshake, and

171

while I was considering how best to thank him, was gone. I sank back into the chair, lost in thought. In the caverns of my memory, time moved swiftly backwards. The desk and office disappeared from my consciousness.

I was on a damp mattress on the floor of the dank, dark cellar staring in horror at the old tin trunk in the corner and the ambulance man kneeling over it shaking his head, I could feel that sinking nausea in the pit of my stomach as I listened with increasing realisation to what he was telling me. Emptiness and desolation closed the space around me.

I watched my drunk and improvident husband, snivelling and complaining up until the moment he left me, his every gesture freshly impressing upon me his utter worthlessness. Nearby, with renewed anxiety, I saw the baker, standing waiting, endlessly waiting, and the grocer next to him, waiting to be paid.

The nightmarish memories gathered momentum. Now, green slime clung to the dripping cellar wall. The cot by the wall was empty. I delved between the bars, my hand stretching, probing among the cold unoccupied blankets, to the mattress and beyond, finding nothing; emptiness in the cot and emptiness in my heart. My baby was gone. Again I had to bury my daughter in the black gaping earth, a bottomless pit, reaching out, too eager to take her tiny afflicted frame. And there, blotting out all the other terrible images was my baby, my son, my Danny, gone too, gone, I knew not where, displaced by John, a stranger.

Danny! I screamed inwardly, this good fortune should have been yours, for us to share. If only I'd known. But I didn't know. Ah, but John, another thought held me. Yes, John, it must be, as the old lady told me. It was John who'd brought this luck.

'Ruth! Ruth dear. Oh there you are! I do envy you.' Angela entered the office, her practical manner releasing the images that haunted me. 'Do you know, with wages like that, you'll be able to live like a queen?'

I was still clutching the cheque in my hand.

'It's not the money,' I stammered, choking on a surge of emotion tinged with sadness, 'It's the chance to be somebody, to do something with my life, that's what I long for.'

Angela stood beside me and lifted me gently to my feet.

'Go home Ruth. You've been sacked from this job.'

We fell into a tearful embrace, propelled by a profound sense of fellowship, as if partners in a long conflict finally overcome. 'You must start your life afresh, from now,' Angela insisted, her usual no-nonsense attitude quickly reasserting itself.

'Oh Angela, I have so much to tell you,' I hesitated, adding almost in a whisper, 'when the time is right. I'm not ready yet.'

'What!' Angela exclaimed pleasantly, 'You still haven't told me everything?'

'Please Angela, will you trust me? It's not possible to tell anyone everything about yourself. But one day, I'm sure, you will know.'

'I'll do my best to get by 'til then,' Angela laughed, 'Now, get along with you.'

I left the hospital and made my way to a bank, which Angela had recommended could deal with my cheque. Gingerly, I pushed open the heavy door and stood for a long time inside the entrance staring at the counter and the people who sat behind the glass partitions, their embossed plastic name plates propped up in front of them, wondering which one I could ask to deal with my cheque. Many people had business in the bank. They marched purposefully to the desk, wrote confidently or shuffled books, forms and money busily and efficiently, all far too preoccupied for me to dare ask.

At the far end of the counter I spotted a sign marked "Enquiries". Nervously I approached and tapped the button on the counter next to the sign.

'Can I help you?' A tall woman with a welcoming smile arrived to greet me from the office behind the counter.

'I've got a cheque,' I began tentatively, 'and I'd like to cash some money against it.'

'I expect you'd like to open an account then. If you wouldn't mind waiting for a moment I'll arrange it for you,' the lady said without waiting for me to explain further.

A couple of minutes later a man approached from my side of the counter and ushered me into a large plush office. Apart from his dark business suit, he was otherwise rather undistinguished. He made sure that I was comfortably seated and introduced himself as the bank's manager.

'What kind of account would you like?' he enquired courteously.

''I'm er not sure,' I dithered, holding out the cheque, 'I'd like an account that would allow me to draw some money straight away.'

The bank manager looked at the cheque and nodded approvingly.

'An ordinary account will do the trick nicely. We don't usually allow money to be drawn against a cheque unless it's been cleared and that takes three days, but I don't expect that this one will cause any problems. I'll attend to the paperwork immediately, just let me know how much you'd like to take now,' he offered.

The bank manager gave me a piece of paper and directed me to the cashier's window. Here I was given several packets of crisp new banknotes, which I placed respectfully in the deepest part of my handbag.

Instead of taking my usual route home, I directed my steps to the bus which would deliver me to the ghetto where resided the very poorest of the town's inhabitants. Nothing seemed to have changed. My flesh crawled with the recollection of how I had suffered in this place and I had to brace myself to ignore the terror I harboured that I would get stuck here, like a fly trapped in a spider's web.

I stood on the road, which led straight to the basement room. To my left was the bakery. In my mind's eye I could see the scene that morning when the baker came to ask for the rent.

"We haven't got anything," shouted Jack.

"Now yer kid's gone it'll be easy t' get yer out o' my property," the baker threatened.

I saw again a lump of wood in Jack's hand and him raising it in the air ready to bring down on the baker's head. After that, we did not see the baker again.

I found the baker without any trouble, standing next to his oven, sweat glistening on his bald head and trickling down his face, looking just the same as on the day I had first encountered him. His eyes darted from side to side when he saw me as if he were expecting something unpleasant. I handed him one of the packets of new banknotes. He looked in astonishment at the money, which was more than my husband Jack and I owed him. I turned to leave. The baker ran after me and tapped my sleeve.

'Oh thank yer and G'bless yer. 'E must've sent yer. Times as bin so 'ard. Those people who took yer away said I was never t' use that room agin, not fer people, not ner animals, ner even t' keep flour. I nearly 'ad t' close the business. Ah, yer dunno 'ow much I need this. G'bless yer. Yer a nice gel.'

Deep in my heart I knew that His blessings were already being heaped upon me. I hurried away, intent on completing my own business and getting away from that horrible place with all its bitter memories.

I made my way to the corner grocery store, satisfied that I had left the baker full of goodwill. The shopkeeper looked at me blankly.

'I'm Ruth,' I offered, 'I used to live here.'

His eyes registered a flicker of recognition. I opened my bag and gave him a large bundle of money.

'This is the money my husband owes you,' I explained.

'Well, thank you,' he looked stunned, 'Er, why?'

'I'm sorry, I can't stay,' I interrupted apologetically, seeing that he meant to ply me with questions and remembering that he was always excessively voluble with his customers.

'Just a minute,' he called me urgently, 'There's too much here. Let me look in my credit book.'

'It's all right. I'm sure there's plenty of interest due after all this time and in any case, you deserve some recompense for all the aggravation and upset we caused you.'

In a moment he had lifted the counter and was standing next to me pumping my hand warmly, effusive with gratitude. 'Please come here and buy again. Don't worry about the past. I'll be so pleased to have you for a customer.'

My heart swelled with contentment, proud and happy that I had brought these people some happiness, glad that I was able this once to be the way I always wanted to be. I was only just able to gulp back the salty tears that fought for release in my throat and eyes.

'Thank you, but I don't live here any more,' I explained as gently and solemnly as I could manage, 'and I really must go now. I'm terribly late, goodbye.'

CHAPTER 11

I had been out much longer than I had realised. Ellen greeted me with a huge sigh of relief.

'Oh Ruth, thank goodness! I was worried.'

'I'm so sorry Ellen. You're right, it's not like me to be late without giving you any warning. It was thoughtless of me not to realise you would worry, but I've had quite a bit of excitement,' I explained, 'I've been offered another job. I'll be paid, so that means I'll be able to give you money too. But first I had to pay all my outstanding debts. That's where I've been.'

'It's OK Ruth, as long as you're all right.'

'You'd better go home now Ellen. Don't worry about coming tomorrow. I won't be at work again until the course starts. And thank you. I don't know how I'd manage without you.'

I went straight to bed, exhausted by the dramatic events of the day. I slept deeply and would have slept late, but early the next morning the telephone rang.

'Ruth, are you all right?' Mark demanded, his voice suffused with anxiety. 'Where were you yesterday? I've been so worried. I'm ringing now because you ought to be leaving for work shortly.'

'I've been sacked!' I exclaimed lightly.

'What!'

'I've been sacked,' I repeated, concealing my meaning a moment longer, 'And I've got some wonderful news to tell you,' I blurted out.

'How can you have good news if you've been sacked? Ruth, you're not making any sense. Tell me what's happened.'

'No, not now,' I said mischievously, 'There's too much to explain and I'd like to try and get some more sleep.'

'Very well, I'll take you out to dinner tonight and you can tell me then. And you don't have to worry about John. Vicky has already offered to baby-sit any time we need someone to look after him. I'll bring her round when I come to collect you.'

'Thank you Mark, that will be lovely. I'll see you later.'

Mark blew a brief kiss into the receiver. I returned the kiss amiably.

A surge of sympathy and warmth claimed my spirit. He's so concerned for me, so sweet, so thoughtful. Perhaps this relationship does have some future? I considered this momentarily, banishing the thought as the image of Mark's father, the high court judge with great status in society, loomed overbearingly and deflated my presumptuous notions.

Early in the evening a shiny red sports car drew up outside the entrance to the block of flats where I lived. The car had a clean straight outline, which gave it the impression of being the ultimate vehicle of transport, like the chariot of some futuristic Pharaoh. Its wide smooth bonnet curved gracefully towards the ground, although the nose of such a splendid conveyance deserved to have been swept upwards into the air.

Vicky was driving, with Mark her passenger and her beautiful son Gary strapped into the baby seat behind. Mark got out and leant into the back to unstrap Gary, while Vicky collected the colourful plastic nursery bag with Gary's things. I waited for them at the top of the utilitarian staircase, which led to my ordinary flat.

Vicky reached the front door first and almost bounced straight through into the lounge.

'How lucky you are Ruth!' she said cheerfully as she greeted me with a friendly peck on the cheek, 'You have everything here; a place of your own, no-one to tell you what to do or to stand in your way. I am envious of you.'

'Vicky, am I hearing right?' I exclaimed.

I wanted to tell her that she didn't know what she was saying. I wanted to tell her how wrong she was. She had no idea what my life was like. Why, she had educated, liberal parents, a brother who was understanding and caring and a home that provided all the material comforts and luxury a person could wish for. And above all, she was surrounded by love from every quarter, love whose very essence I could not even imagine, for I had never had such love from my family nor could ever hope it to be mine. But I decided to leave these sentiments in my own thoughts for the time being, leaving their expression, should they need voicing, to another time.

Mark took me to dinner in a restaurant that had a lovely garden so that patrons could eat in the open air on those long warm sensuous summer evenings that were too inviting to be spent indoors. We chose a table in a sheltered nook near the perimeter greenery. The air was fragrant with the scent of honeysuckle.

'Now Ruth, you can explain. What do you mean telling me you've been sacked?' Mark asked once we were sitting comfortably.

'I've got much more to tell you and you've been so patient. I'm sure you'll agree it was worth waiting to hear.'

I launched excitedly into the story of my unexpected interview, savouring with each word Mark's expressive and appreciative reactions.

'That is truly wonderful news Ruth. You were right. It was worth waiting all day for. I am very impressed, but I can't say I'm surprised. I've always known you were a talented girl, only no-one else has recognised that until now.' Mark brimmed with pride for my achievement, immensely glad that he was sharing it with me.

After dinner we escaped to the park and spent the rest of the breathlessly lovely evening amid the trees under the faint light of a new moon, cuddling playfully, whispering compliments and delighting in innocent larks. We explored kisses that imparted countless delectable sensations, carrying us away on soft clouds of expectancy and tremulous anticipation that reminded me of the times I spent with my soldier Danny.

Vicky was at the door to greet us on our return to the flat.

'Shhh,' she whispered, putting one finger to her lips, 'at least one of the little fellows is fast asleep.'

'That's John isn't it?' I guessed, 'I expect him to be asleep at this hour.'

Vicky nodded, affirming my statement of the obvious, and led the way into my lounge. Gary was sitting on the floor, still wide awake, thanks to his active and inquisitive nature, and delighting in his unusual surroundings.

'He seems happy enough now, long past being tired, but I can't help thinking what you'll have to put up with in the morning. I'm sorry we're so late. We've kept poor Gary up,' I apologised penitently, feeling guilty that I had inadvertently caused Vicky any bother.

'That's all right Ruth. Don't look so upset. Gary's a late bird, just like me and we get up late together,' Vicky reassured me, 'Do you know how many times I leave Mark to baby-sit for Gary and quite often don't come home at all? One good turn deserves another. You've given me some leverage for the future.'

My guilt assuaged, I helped Vicky pack up Gary's things and carried him down to the car.

All night long, questions concerning Mark hovered in the conscious part of my mind. During all those moments when the sleeping brain rose to the brink of consciousness, his influence on my thoughts was unremitting. Even in the morning he was constantly interrupting me in the practical daily tasks I attempted to complete, giving me little rushes of excitement every time I thought of the life of contentment and security I might lead with him. Sense barely held its ground, with its unpalatable practical considerations among a deluge of fantasy.

Ruth, you are being ridiculous. You have let your ideas run wild with you. You know you don't belong. You are just not in their class. I resolved to be strong and think of Mark only as a friend and no more.

After work, the telephone rang.

'Will you come and spend the weekend at my home?' Mark, who knew nothing of my resolve, had just made the very proposal that I should avoid.

I chewed anxiously on my lower lip, my thoughts racing to find the right reply.

'I don't think I can. I'm starting the training course for my new job next week. You know Mark, I've still so much to do,' I said, trying to find a gentle excuse not to meet his parents. Mark was silent. 'And I'm shy to meet your father and mother,' I added.

'That's exactly why I'm inviting you, so that you can meet them.'

'Meet your parents?' Apprehension made me hold my breath. 'No, I can't do that,' I refused outright.

'Ruth, my father only wants to get to know you. He says that he also has an unmarried daughter with a child and it is not so risky for you to meet him.'

'Your father said that, exactly?' I asked incredulously.

'Yes, I promise, that's exactly what he said.'

'Did you tell him anything about me?' I picked up the pen that sat on the notepad by the phone and began to doodle restlessly.

'I told him that you have a baby and, of course, that I like you, no more.'

'Your father sounds very understanding.'

'He is and he's very sensible,' Mark declared firmly, pausing for a moment. 'I'll come and collect you then?'

'Er, em, I'm not sure. Mmm, oh, OK Mark,' my resolution just dissolved away under the influence of Mark's persuasive charm.

On Friday evening Mark collected us in his car. He drove slowly, calm and unconcerned about his family's reaction to me. I sat next to him fiddling nervously with the clasp of my handbag. I remembered how nervous I had been on my first visit to his house. Why had I worried so much? What I now face is so much more daunting, I thought.

'Ruth, you must come and make yourself comfortable in the lounge,' Mark's parents received me warmly, 'Vicky will join us in a moment,' his mother guided me to the best armchair, 'Bring the little fellow in. Sit down.'

'Please don't be shy,' his father urged, 'We don't indulge in unnecessary ceremony with our friends. We want you to feel at home.'

Not a hint of prejudice sullied our meeting. Despite myself, I did feel quite at home. Mark's father, the judge, joked easily with me. He lifted John from my arms and sat him on his knee, 'Hello John. You're a fine fellow aren't you,' he said, playfully bouncing him just like a doting grandfather.

'Well now, here's a singular curiosity,' he said, contemplating John's features closely, 'This child bears no resemblance to you. I cannot imagine that anyone who did not know would perceive him to be your son.'

I felt the colour drain instantly from my face as blind panic and fear gripped me. For a seemingly endless moment I thought, he knows! He's not a judge for nothing. He knows instinctively and now he's interrogating me.

I am certain that his father had dominant genes,' the judge continued conversationally, apparently unaware of my confusion, 'which would of course explain his blue eyes and his skin tone, which is much fairer than yours.'

The judge had drawn attention to an aspect of John's appearance that I had first noticed in the hospital when Josephine had remarked how similar our babies looked. Not for nothing had I wondered then why my genes were so weak. I was only aware that he looked like my baby Danny. My Danny, of whose fate I knew nothing.

Tears welled up in my eyes, urging me to rush from the room so that I might shed them in full flood. No, no, you mustn't, I told myself inwardly, forcing the telltale sobs back from whence they came. You've got to fight these feelings, control your emotions. You mustn't let them affect you. You will have to get used to it.

I can only assume that Mark's father must have taken my silence for embarrassment for he made no further comment. He was kindness itself, a benign gentleman. Once I realised that he bore me nothing but good will, his sympathetic and relaxed manner allowed me to feel completely at ease. It was obvious to whom Mark owed his generous disposition, for his father even complimented me on my new position with its additional responsibility and generous salary.

The judge poured each of us a long cool drink with ice, lemon and a touch of alcohol lacing a fruity cocktail whose origin I could not quite discern. He gently directed most of the conversation, whilst Mark's mother said little, breaking her silence only to relate an occasional anecdote, to enquire as to my comfort, or to wonder aloud when the meal might be ready. At last her impatience got the better of her.

'Will you excuse me, Ruth dear, I must see chef and find out what's happening.'

She returned almost immediately, at the same time as a butler arrived and summoned us to dinner with a grand flourish.

I was prepared for a lavish table, but the display that greeted me in the dining room quite took my breath away. The beautiful olivewood dining table seated twelve with ease. It was carved by hand and very old, sedately presiding over the room with old-fashioned majesty. Its surface was French polished to a smoothness that picked out the sweeping whorls and fine lamination of the olivewood grain, and to a shininess that reflected the image of everything placed upon it. At precise wide intervals around the table were five white damask place mats, each with a distinctive hand embroidered motif upon which rested sufficient heavy silver cutlery for at least four courses. An olivewood sideboard, hand carved and polished like the table, bore cold dishes impeccably presented on ornate silver plates and salvers. Twelve olivewood armchairs upholstered in a rich olive green fabric surrounded the table, completing the magnificent scene. The most pampered of kings could not have expected more.

'Ruth would you like to sit here next to Vicky?' Mark ushered me to my place and pulled the chair out for me so that I could sit comfortably, 'I'm going to sit opposite you,' he whispered.

The liveried butler followed us into the room and stood next to Mark's father who had taken his place at the head of the table. His wife sat opposite him.

The butler took a bottle from a large silver bucket in the centre of the table. He wrapped a spotless white napkin around it and poured some wine for Mark's father. The judge sipped lightly from his tall cut glass goblet.

'Mmm, this is just right. You may serve the wine now please, Samuel,' he turned to me solicitously, 'Samuel has come to us for the evening. We often ask him to help on special occasions.'

Mark's father was evidently a connoisseur of good food and wine, for the meal, from hors d'œuvres to dessert, was crammed with mouth-watering delicacies, the hallmark of cordon bleu cookery. The wines were delicious with the hint of a wooden barrel, light and delicate on the palate without the slightest trace of roughness.

'The food is wonderful and the wine compliments it perfectly,' I said quietly, wanting to show my approval, but uncertain whether it was appropriate to comment.

'I'm delighted that you appreciate the wines, my dear,' replied the judge smiling broadly, 'Over the years I have put down quite a large cellar of my favourite wines and those I have been assured by connoisseurs are excellent. I am afraid I am unable to keep in check my inclination to acquire the best wines that I have had the good fortune to encounter.

'Oh father, you know you are a connoisseur yourself, 'Mark chipped in with some pride, 'and we have Jean-Louis to thank for the meal. Dinners have been pretty special since he's been with us. Come to think of it, his breakfasts and lunches are pretty good too.'

The chef, Jean-Louis, was, I gathered, a permanent member of the household.

Without warning, in striking contrast to my present surroundings of affluence, visions of my own family and the poverty of my early life burst into my mind. The pictures lingered, vividly stirring all manner of disturbing thoughts, my younger brother and sisters whom I had not seen for such a long time but who still might need me; my brother with whom I had been so close. This is the first time that I am not completely preoccupied simply with surviving, I realised. Why now? Just when I have the opportunity to bask in a little luxury, here is my brain, with its perverse machinations, bringing me back to my family. Things are so much better for me now. I must go and see them. I have put off seeing them for too long. I could think of little else.

I realised too that I had postponed telling Mark about my family, reluctant finally to face him with the ultimate truth about me and burst the bubble that I had allowed to carry me away. But he shall know, I will tell him now, everything about them, and that I mean to see them. He will know as soon as we have a moment alone.

Much later in the evening, when Mark's parents finally retired to bed and Vicky too had gone upstairs, declaring cryptically that she was sure we would like to be left alone, my opportunity presented itself. I told Mark all about myself, my family and my home background. Mark sat listening attentively, his face taking on a longer and longer frown of concern.

'Ruth, leave John here with Vicky and first thing in the morning we'll go and find them,' Mark declared with unaffected practicality.

'No Mark, you needn't do that. I don't think it's a very good idea for you to come with me,' I replied without hesitation.

Mark had absorbed my explanation like an amoeba absorbs its food, as part of the natural train of life, but I remembered my family as I had last seen them. My father was an incurable drunkard, my mother was a broken woman and my brother and sisters did not have one pair of decent shoes between them. I wanted to spare him the final reality.

'I love you Ruth,' Mark insisted, breaking into my thoughts, 'and I'm going to marry you. Nothing is going to stop me!'

'Look Mark, I may have to take responsibility for looking after my brother and sisters,' I began to explain. Mark was a very understanding person, but I could not expect him really to understand something so far removed from his own experience.

'I've already told you I want to adopt John. I don't mind looking after your brother and sisters as well.'

Mark made his offer with so much enthusiasm it was hard to believe he had only just heard of the problem.

I don't think you realise what you'd be taking on. I don't think you know who you are talking about,' I countered gently but firmly.

'I know all I need to know and that is sufficient for me. Nothing will change my feelings for you. I've been feeling them since the very first day I saw you.'

'Love!' I laughed loudly, 'If that is true, that you loved me from the first time we met, well I'm sorry Mark, but you don't know what love means.'

'Please Ruth,' Mark pleaded, making a deliberate effort to dampen his own exuberance and match my mood, 'Let me come with you. Please! I promise I will not interfere.' Mark's face bore a meltingly soulful look.

'Oh all right,' I allowed, thinking that this would be the best way to test his love and stop him living in his dream world, 'but only if Vicky offers herself to look after John.'

Of course my condition did not present a problem. Vicky was always the most willing babysitter.

We set out bright and early the next morning for the town of my birth, which was about an hour's journey by the main road. Each minute that Mark drove seemed like three to me for I was preoccupied with my memories and full of apprehension.

After what seemed like an eternity, we reached the outskirts of Hopetown. Every particle of my experience, every ounce of judgement screamed at me to tell Mark to turn back, to run away from the place. Get away, escape what your past will do to you. It has done enough damage.

I looked at Mark for the thousandth time since our journey began. He was calm and unconcerned as he had been all along. No hint of surprise or disappointment crossed his features as we passed into the poor district of the town near my old home. Perhaps, I thought with some irony, it is Mark who had the spirit of Danny and not my baby.

'Mark, have you been here before?' I asked impetuously.

'No, I've never been here. But I have heard all about the area's problems. You know I read the papers. It is often mentioned in the crime columns. Car theft, rape. burglary, they are serious problems here aren't they?'

'Er, yes,' I affirmed, giving Mark more directions, still bemused by his matter of fact attitude.

We found the place where I had lived. but only by association, as a blind man finds his way by force of habit.

If Mark was not shocked when he saw my street, and he appeared not to be, I was. Little remained of the house to evoke any kind of memory, even bad ones. There were no windows, nor even the shape of windows, just gaping holes. The makeshift roof had long since given way and building rubble littered the floor. No-one could possibly live there any more. And it was not just the house that we found neglected, the whole area was derelict and seemed to be completely deserted.

I was quite at a loss, wondering what had become of my family and the neighbours. I began to circle the area, hoping to find some clue, someone who could tell me what had happened. Fortunately, in the wreckage of a house not far from what had been my house, I encountered a young man digging in the rubble. collecting good bricks and other materials that might be used again.

'Do ye want somethin' love?' the man smiled when he saw the expensive car and Mark, who was turned out immaculately as usual, 'Ye don't look like ye belong round 'ere.'

I told him my family's surname and explained that I was looking for them.

'I'm afraid I ain't 'eard of 'em and I dunno anyone round 'ere. But one thing I know, and that's the council moved everyone who was 'ere to another place. It's a few miles away.'

'What do you mean?' I exhorted him, 'what's happened to them?'

'Oh, they all live in beau'iful houses in Matalon. We're the only ones who've bin left 'ere, the ones as c'n look after 'emselves.'

I knew the man was exaggerating when he described the new houses, but I remembered too that all the time I was growing up, my family had the idea, the hope, that one day we and all the neighbourhood would be moved to a civilised place.

Mark drove me to Matalon. The new housing development proved easy to find. Everyone we stopped spoke of it with pride, seeming to be glad to play host in their area to such well designed architecture. The estate was separated from the surrounding houses by wide lawns and communal gardens. The accommodation was in groups of pleasant looking blocks of flats, which would have been taken, at very least, for villas by the people who had been brought there.

One person knew my family and told us where to find them. We drove straight to the block of apartments. A few people had congregated at the entrance to the flats, passing the time of day in idle chatter. I enquired whether anybody knew my mother and father and exactly where I could find them.

'Yes, love,' one large lady answered, 'you'll find 'em up there on second floor,' she waved her arm vaguely in an upward direction.

'It's number 11,' an elderly man made the exact location clear, 'they're usually at home,' he added helpfully.

We climbed two sets of short open stairs. My mother opened the door of the apartment and stood back, looking at me, speechless for a moment in surprise and amazement. Now she almost looked like a skeleton, much thinner than ever before and her skin had become creased and wrinkled.

'Ruth! How lovely to see you! You look so well,' she stepped forward to give me a quick hug and a kiss, 'Come in, come in and bring your friend with you,' she invited, noticing Mark for the first time.

'This is Mark,' I explained as he stepped in behind me.

Despite outward appearances, once inside the flat I realised that nothing much else had changed. There was very little furniture in the main room, only a table and chairs and an old sideboard. The table was spread with nuts, which my mother had been sorting in the same way as she had always done when we were living in the old house. The nuts were the same kinds that we had all eaten then and were the mainstay of our diet. They were one of the better things about our old life, for they had given us some strength and kept us healthy. In another room, I could hear heavy snoring and realised that it was my father, still lying in bed sleeping off a hangover as he had always done.

'Mum, I'm so sorry I've not been to see you for so long. I've wanted to come but ….,'

'It's all right Ruth, you don't have to explain,' my mother interrupted me, 'Life's hard for us all. I know what you went through. I'm sure things haven't been easy,' she indicated the chairs, 'Sit down and we can catch up a bit.'

'I went to the old place but no-one lives there any more. What happened?' I asked, before she had a chance to ask me about Mark.

'We're here because of what Danny did for us,' my mother's face took on a thoughtful expression, 'You remember how hard he fought with the council to get us moved. Well, with bringing the attention of the council to us, they moved everyone. us and all the neighbours as well. They should have named this place after him,' her expression became profoundly sad.

I looked at Mark, wondering what he was thinking. and wanted to tell him all about Danny. but a bitter flashback into the past prevented me from saying anything. Danny was in the coffin and I was standing over it shouting accusingly that he had let me down. He didn't let me down after all, I thought. He's my guardian angel watching over me. My emotions under strain, I felt like shouting at the top of my voice to whoever could hear me that I had given away the baby that Danny gave me. But I didn't. for who would understand and what could they do about it, even if they did?

My mother told me that my younger brother and sister had been placed in a children's home where they received special education outside the mainstream school system. The place was designated for orphans, but some children who faced particular hardship were also placed there to give them an opportunity to study that they would not otherwise have.

The older of my sisters came in with a boyfriend while we were sitting chatting.
'Ruth!' she rushed up to me for a huge cuddle, 'It's great you're here. Are you going to stay?'

I explained to her as best I could why I had come and offered to take the family shopping. We all went together since the children were at home for the weekend. It gave me an enormous amount of pleasure being able to buy them the essential things that every family should have, the things that would have made my life so much more comfortable when I lived at home. I apologised again for not having been in touch for so long, but everyone was too interested in the things we bought, especially the chocolate for the children and personal items for everyone, to worry about my apology or question me further. The day was a tiring one, both physically and emotionally for all of us, but it was a happy and satisfying one too. We said our farewells and promised to see each other again soon.

As we left the building I studied Mark's face to detect his reaction to the events of the day.

'You see, we are not suitable for each other,' I remarked, 'Our backgrounds just don't match. Even if I love you, I can't see that it will work.' I felt certain that after encountering the full truth about me, he could not help but agree with me now.

Hearing the word 'love', Mark stopped and looked at me with deep feeling.

'I've already decided to speak to my parents about my future with you. You are my girl and I want you in my life for good,' he told me warmly.

'Don't be silly Mark. You mustn't tell them anything now. Please, at least give them time to get to know me,' I pleaded. I wanted to be able to enjoy some time with him, before his parents persuaded him to throw me out of his life altogether.

CHAPTER 12

On the Monday following the weekend I presented myself for the course. It was being held in a huge modern office building in the centre of town. A short flight of three or four steps led up to the entrance, which was entirely fabricated from wide glass panels, skilfully joined to give the impression of a vast space inside. The building and its entry looked so impressive that I could not imagine where inside there could possibly be a place for me and I turned round intending to head for home.

"Ruth, you are such an intelligent girl. Have you forgotten how many people, as well as me, think that? You can do so much with your brain if you have the opportunity. And this is your opportunity," Danny's voice sounded from somewhere behind me.

His words encouraged me to carry on. I entered the elegant revolving doors that led into a light and airy foyer. In the middle was a large semi-circular desk made from very pale polished wood. A complicated switchboard was set-up on one side and a large black visitors' book lay open in the middle. A rather overweight man wearing thin wire headphones and a mouthpiece sat behind the desk, near the switchboard. He had a large file in front of him.

'Can I help you miss,' he asked most pleasantly and politely, before I had a chance to ask anything myself. I told him that I'd come for the course.

'Thank you miss, I'll need your name to sign you in.'

'It's Ruth,' I offered.

'And your surname?' the receptionist prompted.

Now I encountered a dilemma. What name should I give? Should it be my husband's name, or Mark's, or Danny's, whose? I didn't want to give Jack's name and I wasn't entitled to give either of the others.

I hesitated. 'What name have they got me down under?'

'You don't know your surname?' he asked in surprise,

'I don't know which one to give you,' I explained.

'You don't look old enough to have had more than one name, but I'll look for Ruth.' He began to run his finger down the list of names.

Then I realised that they must have the name I used in the hospital, my maiden name and I gave him that.

My mind continued to contemplate surnames, wandering into the rosy world I might inhabit if ever I was to take Mark's surname. While I was so preoccupied, the receptionist behind the desk prepared a name badge for me. As well as my name, the card indicated the title of my course and a special identity number registered to me for the duration of the course. The man placed the card in a plastic sleeve, attached a two-way clip and showed me how to fasten it to my clothing.

'You must make sure that you wear this badge all the time you are in the building,' he explained, 'otherwise you won't be allowed in. So please make sure that you don't lose it.'

I wore the badge proudly on the lapel of my jacket, feeling that I had joined the ranks of the educated classes.

'You have to go to the first floor, room number 15,' he remarked helpfully, 'You can use the stairs if you like, its just on the left, but, ooh, yes, you can use the lift,' he repeated, looking at my slight form, 'You don't need to use the stairs, but I always try to use them.' His remarks obviously referred to his own attempts, by not using the lift, to lose some of the excess weight he was carrying. He smiled cheerfully at me as I made my way towards the lift.

I waited for the lift and after it had deposited me on the first floor, I surveyed my surroundings keenly. The whole building resembled a hotel, like the ones I had visited on my holiday with Nelson. It was spacious and light, with sumptuous deep pile carpets in the upper hallways and translucent marble-like tiles on the floor in the reception area. It's so luxurious, I thought, surely I am progressing too quickly?

As I walked along the hallway, I passed five or six numbered rooms. The door of one room stood ajar and I could see a large conference table with seating for 20 or more people. There was a long green baize cover on the table, two pretty flower arrangements and some empty plates and glasses of water. The chairs were scattered around the table in an untidy fashion, giving the impression that the room's occupants had only just vacated it. There are at least five of these rooms here and more at the end of the hall, how many people does this building accommodate? I wondered.

Room 15 was closed, but I noticed a waiting area at the end of the hall and took a seat there. After a few minutes, a young woman in a black skirt and blouse with a white apron and cap approached me.

'Would you like a cup of coffee?' she asked.

For a moment I was about to refuse, even though my mouth was dry with the excitement and apprehension of this new experience.

'It's all part of the service,' the lady added lightly, noticing my hesitation, 'and you don't have to finish it,' she smiled, 'So, shall I fetch you one?'

'Yes, thank you, that will be nice,' I nodded, still rather bemused.

More people began to arrive as I was drinking my coffee. Almost everyone carried something with them, files, papers, books and briefcases. Some of them seemed to be a lot younger than me and I supposed that they were college students sent here as part of their own courses. A few of the people even had small suitcases with them, which struck me as rather odd. I know this place looks like a hotel, I thought, but I didn't think it was one! Each person wore their own identity card like mine.

An older man took the seat next to mine.

'Which class do you belong to?' he enquired in a friendly manner.

I looked at him with a quizzical expression. What does he mean? I didn't know what to answer and I felt stupid.

He looked at my badge, ignoring my puzzlement.

'Oh, I see you belong to class 15. I'm in that class too this week. I've been here for three weeks now. Its part of a six-month course for me.'

I felt embarrassed to tell him that I had only just arrived and that I only came to study for three weeks.

'Why have some people here brought suitcases with them?' I changed the subject and posed him another question.

The man looked surprised by my question and paused for a moment.

'Some people have been at home for the weekend and have come straight here, instead of going first to the accommodation they use while they are on the course,' he explained helpfully, 'They'll take their suitcases there this evening. Some of them stay in hotels or guesthouses. I'm in a hotel myself and my company pays the expenses.' I was listening intently so he went on. 'I've been an engineer for three years, repairing most of the company's machines. Now I'm doing an extended period of advanced training and I'm taking this part of the course, as I usually do from time to time, to keep up to date with all the latest technology.'

'I've only come to study for three weeks,' I told him quietly.

'Yes, you're Ruth!'

I looked at him in surprise. How did he know? Then I remembered my name card, which he had already looked at.

'I know about you already. We have a notice board at work. There's always interesting snippets of information there, news about the company and so on, so most of us make it our business to look at it regularly. A few times now they've posted up a cutting about you from the newsletter of the hospital where you work. It seems that you are an adept problem solver and just the person that we need in times of emergency!'

I was amazed that anybody at all knew about me, never mind important engineers and hospital administrators. It made me feel so proud. I looked at my neighbour's name card to see what his name was, but all that was printed was 'Engineer 25'.

'There's no name on your card!'

'The rooms are ready,' a smart young lady appeared, 'You can make your way to your classes now,' she announced.

Everyone began picking up their belongings and moving to their classrooms. We both stood up too.

'My name is Danny,' the man stated easily.

I froze still in my tracks momentarily and looked at him again. This was Danny? This man was how Danny would come to help me! I searched for some resemblance or indication that he could be Danny, but there was absolutely nothing. We carried on to the class and again Danny sat next to me. While he opened the file he carried and put some papers out in front of him, I looked at him again for any sign of my Danny. No-one could have been more different. He wore very thick glasses, a moustache that didn't suit him and was prematurely bald. On closer examination, I realised that he wasn't much older than me after all and only his features gave the impression of middle age. But even so, he was much too old to be Danny reincarnated. He just wasn't a bit like Danny. How could I bring myself to call him Danny?

My problem was resolved when I noticed that he had written the name 'Dan' at the top of his file of papers. Thank goodness, I thought, I'll call him that.

The class began and at first, never having attended anything like it, I found it hard to follow. Dan was so solicitous of me, explaining some of the technical terms and making sure that I understood what the lecturer was telling us, that I was able to keep up and not to feel too stupid. But by the end of the day, there had been so many new ideas to absorb and so much information was whizzing round in my head that I just wanted to leave the class and never to return. This course and this place are just too far out of my league, I thought. I must not spend any more time or any more of their money on a lost cause.

'It's no good. I can't make it. It's just too difficult for me. I don't think I'll come back tomorrow,' I told Dan with a weary sigh.

He looked at me wide eyed in surprise.

'You can't mean that!' he exclaimed, 'From the impression you've given me today, it won't be too long before you know more than I do. I'm very surprised to hear you talk like this. You have an amazing brain and I feel that I'm learning more from you than you are from me.'

'Why are you laughing at me?' I asked, bewildered.

'I'm not doing that. I'm serious,' Dan reassured me, 'You haven't had the opportunity yet to show how clever you are to anyone else, but I am extremely impressed. Don't forget, I've worked with a lot of people in this area and I know a competent and good worker when I meet one. I think you are wrong to even contemplate not coming back.'

These things were the same things that Danny, my love, had often told me. Again I could hear him telling me. And again I looked at Dan to see if I had missed something and if he resembled Danny in any way. He did not. But Danny had promised to look after me. Perhaps he had chosen this way to do it.

The next day I was amazed by how interesting I found the class and how much I was able to absorb. I made a note of the words that I did not understand and that Dan could not explain while the lesson continued. In the break periods I borrowed a dictionary from Dan to look them up, so that I was able to follow everything that was being taught and was not hampered in my studies.

On the third day we were introduced to some hands-on practical experience, with demonstrations on some mock-ups of the actual machinery and instruments. This part of the course was so interesting that I didn't want to leave at the end of the day, being totally engrossed in the experimental tasks we had been given to solve. Dan had been working all day next to me, but I had only occasionally to ask for his advice.

Everyone else had long gone and Dan packed up his own equipment.

'Come on Ruth, it's time to go home now.'

'Do I have to? I'm just getting the hang of this,' I protested, anxious to practice further my new-found skills.

'Yes, I'm afraid you do. If we hang around here any longer, we'll get locked in the building. Even if we don't want to go home, other people do!' Dan handed me my coat. 'Come on. If you really don't want to go home yet, you can join me for a drink.'

'Oh no, really, I can't. You are right, it is late and I should get home.'

We left the building and Dan walked with me in the direction of my bus stop.

'Look,' he said as we approached the entrance of a small hotel, 'this is where I'm staying. They've got a bar and it's on your way. Why not pop in and have a drink with me? You needn't be long.'

My mind was so full of all I'd learnt that day that a relaxing drink seemed like a good idea, to give my mind a chance to settle before I went home. I rang Ellen and told her I would be a little late.

When I got home later I found a note propped against the flower vase waiting for me.

'I managed to persuade Ellen to let me in so that I could leave something for you to enjoy in the kitchen'

I sent Ellen home and hurried into the kitchen to see what awaited me there. The brown paper carrier bag next to the mug rack contained a take-away meal. Mark must have bought it from the Chinese restaurant round the corner.

John was asleep, so I was able to savour my meal quietly and peacefully like an intoxicated person floating on air, without thinking about anybody or anything in particular. When I had finished my meal I spread all my course books out on the bed and began going over all I had learnt so far. Then I carried on my study to the next stage. It was all so interesting. I revised all the new words of the last three days and noted them carefully in a little exercise book that I had purchased specially for the purpose. To these I added some of the words and expressions that Danny, my soldier, had taught me when I was reading some of the books he had recommended. I did not want to miss or forget anything.

Every evening I waited impatiently for the morning so that I could go back to my classes. The days rushed past filled with study, study and more stimulating wonderful study. I hoped that if I got a good report, I might be recommended for a longer period of study. The idea was challenging and exciting, I was enjoying studying so much. Dan continued to be of great help to me. He was so good to me that he felt as close as a brother and he did not make me feel that I owed him anything. I felt so comfortable sitting next to him, learning from him and I grew to have great respect for him. Of course, I could not call him brother, but I was nonetheless extremely grateful for his support.

At the end of the first week I took a test that was designed to assess how much we had learnt and what needed to be emphasised or revised in the following week's lectures. My result amazed me. I gained a very high score, better than many of the other course participants. I could not help feeling that they had muddled up my paper with somebody else's.

'Miss Harries! Ruth!' the class instructor approached me. I was so glad that he called me by my own name and not by Jack's, 'You did very well in the exam this week and that is excellent.' I wanted to tell him that I had found it very easy, but he continued, 'but the machine we focussed on this week was one of the simplest that we have to deal with. I have to tell you that we will be going on to more complex instruments next week. I understand that you are taking this course so that you can take up a position as a peripatetic trouble-shooter for all the hospitals in the area, under the direct supervision of Mr Kleinman. He's very important in the company, but I want you to know that I feel sure that you are capable doing the job well and that you don't need to worry.'

True to the instructor's prediction, I passed the course with flying colours. The course had boosted my confidence immensely. The topics that I had studied there only touched upon the wealth of knowledge that was available and so interested me that I determined to take more classes to further my education. Ellen was a very sensible and kind babysitter, taking care of John with such enthusiasm that she was in some ways better than me. She was so diligent with him that I was not worried about leaving him with her for the extra time when I was taking the evening classes. When I had exhausted the local possibilities for study, I discovered that it was possible to undertake a university course by post, eventually leading to a degree. Insatiable for knowledge, I enrolled and pursued these studies vigorously. In time I moved out of my temporary bedsitting room to a proper flat where John and I had a room each.

My driving lessons too reached fruition in an extremely nerve-wracking driving test, which I need not have worried about as I passed at my first attempt. This allowed me to start driving my own beautiful car. It was a glorious shade of light blue chosen myself from all those displayed in the showroom. It is hard to describe my feelings on acquiring this car and so I will leave it to you to imagine just how exciting this was for me.

In every way it seemed that Danny, my soldier, was looking out for me and encouraging me. My constant regret through all my miraculous change of fortune was that I had changed my baby Danny for John, even though John was a good natured and sweet tempered child. For both our sakes, I convinced myself that my good fortune came from John's own good luck. He had been born into a well to do family and he was the reason that I had found good fortune, to ensure his birthright.

Mark loved children so much, he could have been a father to any child, but he quickly established such a special bond with John that he could have been his real father. I knew that Mark's parents would never accept me as a wife for Mark and I made a mental note not to get too involved emotionally with him, particularly after I heard the remark Vicky made a few days earlier.

'Mum and Dad have got such plans for us for the future!'

If they had plans for Mark and Vicky, I was certain that I did not feature in them.

On almost every occasion that Vicky went out, she asked me to look after Gary for her.

'I want Gary to learn all the things I've seen you teach John,' she said, 'You are so sensible with him.'

Mark took full advantage of these outings to share the babysitting duties and spend as much time as he could with me. Vicky reminded me how lucky she thought I was to have a place of my own and to be independent. This idea was accompanied by Vicky's own contingency plans.

'You know Ruthie, if ever I were to choose a godmother for Gary, it would be you. I can't think of anyone else who would do the job so well.'

Vicky and I had so much in common, in part because of Mark and in part because of John and Gary, that we became the very best of friends. I think it may even have happened without the involvement of Mark, for we had so much to talk about.

CHAPTER 13

Vicky went away on holiday leaving Gary with me.

This was a wonderful excuse for Mark to move in with me, telling his parents that he could not possibly leave me to look after Gary all by myself for a week. For three days we enjoyed the best time that I had experienced since my Danny died. We spent our time like a husband and wife, mother and father, looking after the children. John and Gary were both walking and the three 'boys' endlessly ran about, exploring and playing all manner of madcap and energetic games. I often joined in, but at other times was content just to watch their merriment.

I found myself falling for Mark, but remembered my pledge to myself not to get involved. When I realised this, I took myself off on a little walk, letting fall the tears that pricked my eyes. These were not morbid tears, but tears of release, even hope. Later on I looked at my Danny's picture telling myself, I don't want to fall in love again and be disappointed.

On the third day, we had just returned from the park when the telephone rang. I picked up the receiver.

'Hello.'

'Hello, Mark? Is Mark there please?' It was the voice of Mark's mother. It was very distant and sad.

'Yes, he is,' I replied hesitantly. Her tone quite disconcerted me.

'Can you fetch,' her voice broke off for a moment, choking with emotion, 'fetch him for me please?'

'Yes, just a moment.'

Shaking with apprehension, I held out the receiver to Mark who had heard the uncertainty in my voice and was staring at me with a look of puzzlement. I could still hear his mother's distressed voice.

'Mark? Hello Mark. Hello.'

Mark took the phone.

'Is that you mother?'

'Mark, your sister's been killed. Vicky's dead.'

Standing next to Mark, I could hear the agony in Mark's mother's voice vibrating down the telephone wire. Abruptly the telephone clicked loudly and the line transmitted a low pitched moan. Mark stood rooted to the spot, like a scorpion had stung him. The receiver hung limp in his hand. I took the receiver, replaced it briefly on the handset and dialled Mark's home.

'It's Ruth, I've got Mark here,' I stated hurriedly when the phone was answered and handed Mark back the receiver.

'Vicky has been killed in a motor accident. She and her friend were killed instantly,' I could hear the butler telling Mark.

'Tell mum, er, tell mum I'm, ah, coming straight home. I'll, ah, bring Gary with me.' Mark could barely speak. He stood shaking, speechless with shock. I took the receiver from him again and replaced it.

'Vicky, Vicky's dead,' suddenly Mark's tongue was loosened, 'An accident. She was in an accident. Vicky's dead,' he began repeating himself, like a zombie, over and over again.

Vicky, my friend, I thought. Vicky who was so good to me. Vicky who befriended me and took me into her life. Dead. Vicky, dear Vicky. Why does this happen to the people I love? Why do they all go? This can't be happening. Not again. It can't happen to me. After everything. But I realised that if it could happen to Danny, it could happen to anyone.

I had a strangling feeling in my stomach and wanted to be sick but it went no further. Mark started to retch uncontrollably and was physically sick. He was in no condition to drive and neither was I, so I phoned for a taxi and quickly packed up Gary's things while we waited for it to arrive.

On the way back to Mark's house I confided in him about my soldier.

'I lost someone else very dear to me once,' I began telling him all about Danny's character and relating the story of the bed-wetting episode, when Danny helped my brother and sisters, to illustrate what he was like.

'So you can probably imagine how I felt when he died. That's how I know what you are feeling now. It's all come back to me,' I concluded, as the nightmare scenario replayed itself to me.

Mark was as pale as a ghost, but as he listened to me he gradually stopped retching and looked a little better. He put his arms round me and held me tightly, clinging on to me for support and comfort in a common grief. We sat together like that all the way, me trying to comfort him and he trying to comfort me.

'I do love you so much,' he told me, 'and I'm going to look after you even better now.'

'Please Mark, don't say that,' I pleaded, 'It's what Danny said and you know what happened.'

'Then I promise you, my first son with you will be called Danny,' Mark affirmed as a few tears ran down his face.

I wanted to tell him that I already had a son Danny, but now was not the time or the place nor, for that matter, would it ever be.

At the house, Mark's mother and father were sitting silently together in the living room. They rose as Mark entered and his mother fell on his shoulder sobbing her heart out. I looked on helplessly, as I watched the heart-rending scene. I proffered my deepest sympathy and offered to do whatever I could to help. Mark's father stood silently, drained of all colour and emotion. After a few achingly sad minutes, the judge took charge.

'Ruth, would you mind looking after Gary for a little while longer?'

'No, of course not,' I nodded, glad to have been given something to do.

'If you don't mind doing that, you must stay here.'

'I don't mind. I'd like to,' I assured him.

'Go home and pack some things for yourself and John. Take a taxi. I don't think any of us is in a fit state to drive now, even you. And please keep Gary with you. It will be better if he stays with you at present.'

When I returned an hour or so later a scene of ordered chaos greeted me. Cars littered the approaches to the house and a policeman had arrived to direct newcomers to the best places to park. I got out of the car and was greeted by an unnatural silence. I could not hear any sounds of grief, no crying or wailing or any other sound that I expected to issue from a house of mourning.

Inside the house many people were sitting or standing, talking in hushed tones. The atmosphere was sombre, but no one was crying or demonstrating their loss by loud protestations in the way that would have been normal for the people I grew up with. The chief of police was there, dressed in his uniform, and I recognised one or two members of parliament from having seen their pictures in the papers. All the visitors were attired as if they were attending a business meeting. Even Mark's father and mother appeared to be wearing their best clothes, too good for this occasion. These are the clothes you would wear to a wedding, I thought. Only by looking at their tired and drawn faces could I recognise that this was not a happy occasion. I had hurried to pack and return as soon as possible and had not changed from the clothes I had worn all day, which were very ordinary and shabby by comparison. I felt very shy and embarrassed. What must they think of me? I wondered. Perhaps they will think I am the cleaner's sister or helper. Why had Mark not thought to tell me that I needed to put on my best clothes? I took Gary and John, one in each hand, and made a hasty escape upstairs to the room where such a short time ago I had played with Vicky and the children.

No one had taken any notice of Gary or John. Vicky's image appeared in front of me as I gazed at Gary, wondering what life held in store for this motherless child.

"I love you Ruthie. I am so sorry I've left you. You are the only person I want to look after my Gary. You must be his godmother, just as I told you. I don't want him to stay with my mother."

Vicky was only 21 and, like Danny, her life was over.

The funeral was a stately affair. It provided a fitting and noble tribute to a young woman from a highly respected, well to do family. The mourners gathered in a small modern chapel. They all wore the most respectful attire in smart sombre colours with appropriate black hats, gloves and scarves as accessories. The judge seemed composed, as befitted his position, but only a cursory examination revealed him to be worn out, lines of pain that I had not noticed before etching his forehead. He had aged considerably in a few short days. He must have felt just as I did when Danny died, but he concealed his true feelings behind an expressionless exterior. The ceremony did not take long, but there was time for several dignitaries to make sad eulogies on the theme of life cut short in its prime and the anguish of a parent who must bury a child. They related how clever and ambitious Vicky had been, but no one mentioned Gary.

A grand procession accompanied the coffin to the graveside, led by five or six notable personages in ceremonial garb. Again I found myself by a grave while fresh earth was thrown over my dear best friend. Danny was there, again and again holding me and comforting me as I stood in stunned disbelief. Of course, it was Mark supporting me and in doing so, supporting himself at the same time. But not one tear emerged from my eyes. I suppose that the deaths of Danny and my two daughters had immunised me, leaving me completely spent of emotion.

On our return to Mark's house, all the principal mourners donned black armbands, which they wore over their sleeves as a mark of respect to the memory of the departed. All week long, people came and went so that the mourners were rarely alone. They paid their respects and stayed for a while. Most were upset and sad, but I saw some smiling as they chatted amongst themselves. A few tears were shed, but I saw no one crying and nothing of the terrible hysteria of hopeless misery that I expected. I stayed there all week, making myself useful. And I stayed in the same room where I had spent my very first night in the house and which I had never imagined to occupy again.

Several times while I slept in that room, I dreamed about what Vicky had said to me.

"Ruthie, will you look after my baby if something happens to me?"

It was so strange, the accident taking place so soon after she told me this, almost as if it had been planned. And the dream kept recurring. Mark showed me a postcard that Vicky had sent home from her holiday. It was mostly about a local charity that she had decided to take under her wing. One comment though, glared out at me.

"I am not in the least bit worried about Gary because I know that Ruth is keeping a careful eye on him."

This convinced me that the dream was conveying an important message to me, but I could not think of any way that Vicky's parents would entrust Gary to me.

In a quiet moment during the week that I stayed in the house, Mark's mother approached me.

'Ruth, have you got a minute?' she enquired, 'Can you come with me.'

She took me to Vicky's room. There she opened a door leading to Vicky's dressing room. Along two of the walls hung rails full of clothes. I knew that Vicky had a lot of clothes, because I never saw her in the same outfit more than once. There was something for every occasion, smart, dressy, fancy, casual and sporty, from floor length evening gowns to shorts for the beach. The upper part of the third wall was lined with shelves, for tops, swimsuits, underwear and accessories, like gloves, handbags and scarves. Below the shelves were racks of shoes. These paraded in straight rows, like soldiers in a myriad of uniforms of every colour and shape. I never imagined so many clothes could belong to one person.

'I want you to take everything,' Mark's mother told me, 'Anything that you don't need or can't use, please give to somebody suitable.' she added noting my look of surprise.

'Yes, thank you. I come across a lot of people at work who would be very grateful for these,' I answered.

'I am sure you do, but I would prefer you to take most things for yourself. It's what Vicky would have wanted.'

When she mentioned what Vicky might have wanted, I thought of telling her about my recurring dream, but was not sure that this was the right time or place. She showed no sign of worrying about Gary and his future. It even seemed to me that she felt that it was not for her to worry about him, but I realised that this attitude was probably more the result of extreme grief than from any lack of responsibility.

The end of a very long week arrived. We all sat quietly eating our evening meal. Everybody was gathered together, giving me an opportunity to give voice to another concern.

'I'm afraid that I will have to go home very soon, back to my job. They have been very understanding, but I feel I mustn't press them too hard,' I explained.

'Ruth, I want to marry you,' Mark jumped to his feet, pushing his chair away from behind him, 'Will you marry me?'

I looked from Mark to his father, uncertain what to reply. For a moment I thought that everyone in the room was holding their breath, the silence was so ubiquitous, and that there would be a mass fainting, but nothing happened. The judge's face was particularly impassive.

'Mark, sit down!' his father instructed him, 'Sit down!'

With his usual respect and trust of his father, Mark did as he was told.

'I must tell you Ruth, what our feelings are towards you,' his father turned to me, 'When Mark first brought you to our house, we were happy that he had a friend, someone to spend time with and have fun. Mark has had girlfriends before and has even been passionate about them, but that usually passed and they drifted apart. This is what we assumed would happen with you too. But Mark's relationship with you was not like that. Of course, when we realised that he was genuinely falling in love with you, we thought about trying to stop him.

We wanted to tell him that this was not the right match for him.'

I glanced around at this point, trying to gauge what everyone present was thinking and bracing myself for what I imagined was coming next. "Now you must go home and leave Mark alone. Give him a chance to find someone who will guarantee a good future for Gary."

But the judge continued, looking at me with extreme sympathy, 'Then he told us about the courses you were taking and how you had an ambition to study at university, and we withheld our opinions. We saw that you did take that degree course and were still as keen as ever to continue studying and we felt a great deal warmer towards you and were happy for you both. We have been waiting for Mark to ask for your hand in marriage, but somehow he has not done so until now, perhaps because we haven't told him how we feel.'

'Marriage', did he say 'marriage'? Did I hear right? My thoughts raced off for a moment on their own track and then hurtled back to listen to what Mark's father would say next.

'But now that we have lost our precious daughter Vicky, who, with our son, was the most important thing in our lives, we have no daughter but you.'

'Daughter!' he called me. I burst into tears, and surprised myself at the depth of emotion that engulfed me. Since Danny died I thought the well of my tears had dried up, I had wept so much for him. If I had felt such emotion at the deaths of my two daughters, I had not deferred to it. I could not believe the evidence of my own ears. The high judge, respectable and educated, called me 'daughter'.

The words Danny said as I ached for him at the graveside reverberated through my brain, "I will come back to you, I promise. You must look after yourself".

Mark's father rose from his seat and stretched his arms out towards me. I rose too and went to meet him. 'Ruth, dear,' he whispered, cuddling me and kissing me affectionately on my forehead. I sank into his arms and hugged him tightly for the father I had wanted all my life but did not have until now. I thought I felt a tear drop on to my cheek from his face above mine.

Mark's mother, a handkerchief to her eyes, left her place and hurried from the room. She returned a few minutes later clutching an intricately decorated trinket box.

'This is for you,' she proffered it to me, 'from Vicky.'
I opened the box and music rang out. A lovely melody played to all of us assembled there, surrounding us with love and emotion. I recognised the tune as one of Elvis Presley's enduring love ballads.

'That's one of Vicky's favourite songs,' Mark said, 'I bought it for her eighteenth birthday.'

The box contained all Vicky's most precious jewellery, her favourite gold necklace with the tiny rubies and opals that I remembered her wearing often, and rings, bracelets and earrings, each piece beautiful and so distinctly Vicky's taste.

'Vicky would have wanted you to have this,' Mark's mother continued, 'She was so fond of you. She often said that she could think of nothing better than for you both to live together and bring up your children together.'

'Thank you so much. I would very much like to look after Gary from now on.' I stated confidently, 'Will you let me?'

Mark stood up again, 'Where my sister's child goes, I am going. He's not going anywhere without me.'

The arrangement was tacitly agreed then and there.

A wedding was made for Mark and myself. Mark's parents took on the splendid and complex organisation as if they were making a wedding for Vicky. No expense was spared, exactly as they would have done for Vicky. I was even taken to Vicky's favourite shop to buy the wedding dress and shown what Vicky would have liked, but I did not mind. I knew that they were doing it because they loved me as if I was Vicky.

My mother and father and brother and sisters were all invited. They were each provided with suitable attire for an extremely smart wedding and although we hired clothing for my parents, my brother and sisters had something new. And it was not only their outfits had to be considered. So as not to embarrass themselves or me, we sent the family's friendly butler, Samuel, to give them lessons and tips on behaviour and manners. Even Danny, my soldier, would have found it difficult to attain the standard of behaviour that I expected my family to achieve for the occasion.

Mark came with me to visit Danny's grave.

'This picture is in a fine mess,' Mark said when he saw the sorry state of Danny's photo on the grave, 'We must get a special waterproof frame and seal it from the elements. I'll arrange it.'

I looked at him gratefully and knelt over the gravestone brushing the flat top with a cloth that I had brought for the purpose. I will never forget you, I told Danny silently. Please can you help me to find my son so that I can invite him to the wedding?

I kissed the grave and was amazed when Mark did the same.

As I got up to leave, Mark stood solemnly in front of the grave.

'Danny,' he said, 'I promise you, on my life, that I will look after Ruth just as you wanted to look after her.'

With this special promise uppermost in our thoughts we slowly retraced our steps to the gate of the graveyard. Though part of my heart would forever be with Danny, I felt content with Mark, who, in many ways, was like Danny.

'Ruth, we have found Jack,' Mark explained as we returned home, 'He has signed all the necessary papers without any problem. You are free now.'

Mark looked at me, but I did not take in what he said, my mind was still full of the promises and of Danny and the past.

CHAPTER 14

Both babies came on our honeymoon with us. How much I wanted my baby Danny to be with us too, but by then I already had formed a deep bond of affection with John and begun to love him, alleviating some of my longing. Gary was such a handsome child that he easily endeared himself to me, calling me 'Mummy' even before John did.

We found a wild cascading waterfall in a quiet area inland from the main resort. The children were entranced by the flashing drops of water that hung in the air creating a rainbow spectrum of colours. They adored splashing about in the shallow pool at the edge of the fall where the cooling spray ventured periodically to sprinkle itself on their hands and faces. We spent three whole days there. Who wanted to go home? So we booked another week away.

'The kids are great, but we haven't had enough time together,' Mark said in justification, 'I think we deserve two week's honeymoon.'

My life mirrored that of Cinderella. I was a poor girl with nothing to look forward to and now I had been transformed into a princess. Only one thing stood in the way of my perfect happiness. My baby Danny was not with me to share my good fortune. But I managed to carry on, telling myself that just as Danny was looking out for me, so he would be doing for his namesake, little Danny, too. I remembered once telling Danny that I had not planned what to do with my life.

"How do you make God laugh?" he had asked me.

I shrugged, and looked at him for a reply.

"By telling him your plan," he joked so wisely. Now I knew how right he was.

On our return from honeymoon, Mark gave me some amazing news.

'Ruthie, you're not going back to your old flat, we're not going to live there. I've bought us a home of our own!'

He whisked me off to show me the bungalow he had purchased. It was detached with its own garden, had three bedrooms and was fitted out fashionably with every modern convenience and luxury. Mark had obviously listened with great attention to any hints I might have given him about the kind of things I liked, for I could not fault the choice of décor nor the style of furniture as they matched my own preferences exactly.

'Mark, its fabulous. But how on earth did you afford it?'

'Do you remember the company that sent me to give you the ticket?' he smiled that mysterious smile of his, 'Well, that company belongs to me!'

'What!' I had never guessed, 'I thought you were just working for them.'

'No, it belongs to me. But I didn't want you to marry me for my money.'

'Why didn't you tell me before?' I asked, feeling upset that he had kept me in the dark for so long, 'Money isn't important to me. Mark. I thought you knew that. I didn't marry you for your money.'

Mark shrugged his shoulders, a little bewildered by my reaction.

'But why do you give people their prizes?' I continued, wanting to know more, 'You could employ someone to do that. couldn't you?'

'Of course, I could. I've got 800 people working in the company. But you want to know why do I do it?' Mark tipped his head jauntily to one side and smiled broadly, 'I really enjoy seeing the look on people's faces when I give them the good news. Anyway, I was looking for a wife and behold I found one,' he joked, indicating that was me and that I should come over for a cuddle.

'Tell me the truth Mark,' I had to know one more thing, 'Is it true that the company pays for the taxi to the airport, as you did for me?'

'No they don't, but I knew that you would be my wife and that you would love me more than anyone else. Well, that's true isn't it, at least if we don't talk about Danny who you loved so much.'

Mark did not say this in a jealous or cross way, just as a matter of fact. I took him up on his offer of a cuddle and we hugged each other fondly for the first time in our new home.

Our boys grew up together as brothers, but they were totally different in character as well as appearance. Gary was three months older than John and a boisterous child, full of energy for everything except his schoolwork. He had inherited a lot of Vicky's verve and enthusiasm for all life could offer. We never found out who his father was. Gary did not like to study and it was always an uphill task to get him to do his homework. But he was very good with his hands and often would amaze us with his handiwork in wood or his construction of gadgets, like a homemade radio. He was a handsome boy too who was not shy to take advantage of his good looks and outgoing personality to gain all the attention he required from his friends and family.

John was an entirely different character. He was easy going and good natured, a placid child who willingly went about his studies diligently without being prompted. There was no need to tell John what to do, nor to discipline him, as he understood rules and obeyed them without question. John could not have loved me more, day by day becoming closer to me. I do not think even a natural child could have loved and respected his mother more.

As he grew older, he asked my advice about everything that mattered to him.

'Mum, I find grandpa's discussions of the law so interesting. Do you think I could be a lawyer one day?'

'Mum, which university do you think will give me the best education in law? I've got their syllabuses here. Will you help me look through them and decide?'

'Mum,' he would often say, 'Your heart is mine. If I ever get married, I would like my wife to be just like you.'

So many times when he told me this I wanted to tell him that he was not my real son, but I knew that this could only spoil everything that we had and would achieve nothing but trouble. I would be sent to languish for the rest of my days in prison, losing my love, my home, my children and everything I had achieved. Mark's life would be forever marred by scandal and lies. What a terrible way to repay him for all he had done for me. Mark's parents would be vindicated in their original ideas about me and accuse me of ingratitude. Who could blame them? So I pushed all ideas of revealing the truth to the back of my mind, though the knowledge sat like a time bomb waiting to explode. Mentally I prepared for a huge disruption one day.

Money, or should I say the lack of it, was never again to concern me. I was now in a position truly to help my family. Further education places were arranged for my brother and sisters, with a monthly allowance to help them to maintain their education. I helped them to afford homes of their own when they were ready to earn their own living and to live independently. I found reliable and interesting jobs for my mother and for my father, who had vowed to keep to a standard and not let me down. They also received a monthly allowance so that whatever they earned, they no longer had to worry about the little luxuries that make life comfortable. But they all lived too far away for us to be able to visit very often and our situations were too disparate to have much more than a minimum involvement in each other's lives.

Our bungalow was comfortable and a great delight to me. At last, I had a home of my own that I could be proud of. But the day came when another baby was on the way and the boys were growing rapidly, needing more and more space. We moved into a much bigger and more splendid house just in time for the birth of our own daughter, Victoria.

Inspired by his grandfather, John became interested in the law. He took up the subject seriously as soon the option became available to him at his private school, continuing his studies through university. As with everything John set his mind to, he gained excellent results in all his exams and went on to win a prime legal position in a government department.

'Grandpa,' John had once asked Mark's father, 'You don't need to work any more, why don't you retire? You could take your pension.'

'Ah, lad,' the judge replied, 'Judges don't retire, because as they get older they become wiser and are therefore better at their job. If a judge takes up his pension it usually means that he is creeping into senility and no longer knows what he is doing. Even then, he may have to be persuaded to stand down.'

Time passed in tranquillity and happiness. But I felt that it must be the calm before the storm. The nagging fear never left me that something would happen to shatter the happiness and that I would finally wake up and find that it had all been a dream.

CHAPTER 15

After dinner at Mark's parents' house one day, we retired to the lounge. John came to sit next to me.

'Mum, I've got a problem and I'd be grateful for your advice.'

'What is it John? Is a girl giving you problems?' I enquired affectionately, looking forward to exercising my motherly role.

'No Mum, I wish it were a girl. That would be nice,' he looked at me whimsically, 'No, my problem is a legal one that has arisen at work.'

'All right, darling, I'll do my best.' Now I was more flattered than before. John wanted my advice on a legal problem!

'As you know, I work for the government and have to defend the principles upon which the law is formulated. It has become common practice, in cases where there may be reason to suspect the background and heredity of young couples wishing to marry, but who may inadvertently be very close relatives, to require the use of a blood test to determine or confirm their parentage, in order to protect society and ensure their integrity.

A young doctor is challenging the validity of this blood test. He postulates that the blood test is unreliable and inaccurate and should not have any legal validity in this instance. The medical establishment and the law support the use of the blood test as it is deemed to be one hundred per cent accurate. The doctor says that because it is unreliable, the blood test can provide no reliable proof that a person is clearly the genetic offspring of the mother or father and that public money is being wasted on the blood test.'

'John, I am flattered that you have asked me, but I think you need to ask your grandfather about this. He is the expert and as you say, it is a complex problem.'

Presently the judge joined us, having finished the discussion he was having with Mark that had kept him until now at the dining room table. John approached him and explained his problem again.

'Grandpa,' he finished, 'the doctor has brought scientific evidence proving that the test is invalid. Please can you give me some advice on how to proceed.'

The judge looked at John pensively, considering his answer carefully.

'You know John, any judge worth his salt, the kind who has risen to the lofty heights of the high court, did not reach his position by taking advice from other judges. Those judges attained their high rank because they were good lawyers first and as such they did a great amount of research into the law and its workings. As lawyers, they will have had to find all the relevant past judgements and put forward all the cases where legal precedent could be made. They researched the relevant case law, presenting chapter and verse for the benefit of the judge and to prove their arguments. I think it will be a good idea if you start here,' the judge turned round and indicated the heavy mahogany bookshelves that spanned one side of the room behind him, 'or better still, go into my study and begin doing your research. There are even more books there. Then, when you have a good grasp of the law as it pertains to this matter, you will be able to present your ideas to the judge who will be presiding over your case.

'Thank you grandpa,' John listened solemnly, 'I will do that.'

'I remember when I was a young lawyer,' the judge smiled at John and continued, 'I went to all my friends and asked them if they could help me with a particular problem that was perplexing me. Every one of them insisted that he had a problem far more difficult than mine to solve and I was left to use my own ingenuity to find a solution. '

'What was the case?' Please tell me about it.' John pleaded enthusiastically.

'Very well,' the judge looked at me and then back at John, 'I'll tell you about it.' He made himself comfortable on the sofa, plumping up one of the cushions and positioned it behind his back, turning to face me in the process.

'It was a marital dispute,' the judge began. His face creased momentarily in deep thought as he recalled the details to his mind. 'A husband brought the case against his wife because he argued that he was not the natural father of the child she was bringing up in his home. He wanted a blood test on the child to prove his accusation. I was appointed to represent the wife. I was given the brief a month in advance to do my research and prepare the case. The deeper I went into the case the more I realised how much work would be involved in winning it for my client. My client refused to let the child have the test. Instead, she accused her husband of slander. The law could not be used to force her to allow the test because the husband had provided no evidence to prove his complaint.'

John's grandfather looked at me seriously almost as if he were judging me, jolting me out of my quiet attention to his story. This could happen to my son Danny, I thought to myself. He might face this problem one day. Shall I ask the judge the name of his client? Dare I?

John's grandfather got up from the capacious settee and took down some finely bound books from among the vast array of different books on many subjects that graced the bookshelves.

'These are a few of the books that I used then,' he explained, handing them to John, 'I read them through over and over to obtain the information I needed. It took me weeks during which time I hardly slept and never had a proper meal. If you look into these books John, you too may find the exact case you need. Eventually I found a case where the judge made just the ruling and created just the precedent that I was looking for. It pertained to a dispute ten years earlier. In his summing up, the judge stated that when a couple are legally married, the husband automatically becomes the legal father of any child that the wife conceives. No other man, even if he is the biological father of the child, has any right to ask for a blood test or even to have access to the child if the husband has recognised the child as his own by putting his name on the birth certificate. If there is no proof of any misbehaviour on the part of the wife, neither the husband nor any other man can ask for a blood test. The only circumstance in which a blood test is permitted is if the husband is requesting a divorce.'

John's grandfather returned to his place on the sofa facing me.

'In the court, the husband's lawyer put forward his argument. When he had finished I called the husband to the witness box.

"Do you want to divorce your wife?" I asked him, "Is that why you have accused her of having a child that is not yours?"

"No, sir."

Thank goodness, the man's negative response allowed me to continue.

"Do you have any evidence that the child is not yours? Did your wife fall in love with someone else or go out with someone else? Did you catch her in bed with someone else? Did she say anything to gave you the idea that she did?"

"No, sir, I don't."

I had been afraid that if he answered positively, I would be unable to use all the evidence that I had spent so many weeks collecting and my whole argument would collapse. Now I approached the judge and quoted him the precedent that I had found in the case from ten years previously. The judge gave judgement in the favour of my client.

"As a judge, it is my duty to make clear and fair judgement," he stated in his closing speech to the court, "When attorneys make a well researched argument, as I have heard here today, it becomes easy for me to establish the proper judgement. I am dismissing the case of the plaintiff."

So you see John, if you do your homework well and patiently, you too could be standing before your judge and be told what I was told,' John's grandfather concluded.

John took the books and went straight to his grandfather's study, beginning the serious research of his problem. Like his grandfather had done before him, for two weeks he barely surfaced from his desk. We hardly ever saw him, not for lunch or dinner, so little in fact that I became concerned that he would make himself ill from malnourishment.

John arrived home late from his office one evening. We were having dinner at Mark's parent's house. He sat down at the table looking pale and drawn.

'You look exhausted John,' the judge remarked, 'What's happened?'

'Grandpa, I've looked at all the books you recommended and many more, but I can't find any clue or any similar cases. I need a lot more time,' John said wearily, 'The trouble is the media have got hold of the story. They ran a piece on the local radio and it generated so much interest that the national television news want to run an extended story and interview. I've pleaded with them to hold off for a little longer, but it won't be long before we find ourselves in the spotlight. And I've got no answer to give them.' John sank his head into his hands and closed his eyes in complete dejection.

'Come on lad, you need to eat something. Food feeds the mind as well as the body,' the judge put his arm round John, 'It can't be that bad. After dinner, bring me the details and all the cases you've looked at so far and we will sit and go through it together.'

'Thanks grandpa, I'd really appreciate some input from you,' John looked at him gratefully, 'and Mum, can you come too?' True to form, John wanted some input from me too.

John and his grandfather sat together at his desk in the study and I sat in an armchair listening.

'Grandpa, it's like I told you before, the young doctor, he's actually a haematologist, is challenging the law regarding blood tests. He says it is unreliable and should no longer be used as accurate evidence of parentage. As proof he cites his own blood test and family history. Using current up-to-date blood testing techniques, for which he is an expert, his blood matches that of his father and of his brothers, but it bears no relation whatsoever to the blood of the woman who gave birth to him, his mother.'

John paused while he looked through some documents that he had brought with him and passed one sheet to his grandfather and one to me. It was a laboratory test form, neatly filled in with the results of several blood tests.

'Look, here it is in black and white. We requested that the test be done by an independent laboratory. Their results are exactly the same as the doctor's. Mum's got theirs and you've got ours. You can see for yourselves.'

The judge and I compared documents. They were identical to within the limits of the accuracy of the test.

'These results are only the beginning,' John continued earnestly, 'The mother insists that he is the son she gave birth to. We checked the hospital records and she did give birth to a boy there exactly as she and the rest of the family testify.'

These words stirred up vague recollections in my brain, but I pushed them to one side, thinking, of course, this is standard procedure, of course they checked something like that. It must happen all the time.

'Well,' said the judge, 'I'm not surprised the media are interested. This has huge implications for many people's lives. The legal repercussions will not be insignificant either.'

I wondered if the judge realised that even this bold remark was likely to be an understatement.

'The trouble is that for the moment the main problem remains a medical one. And you feel that the involvement of the television and newspapers will make the case an embarrassment for you?' the judge frowned, 'Evidence John, you have to find some more evidence, medical as well as legal.'

'Yes grandfather, thank you. I know I've got a lot more work to do, and I'll need your support,' John got up slowly and turned to me, 'Mum, I am going to need your help and support more than ever now. Its very important to me.'

Only the next day, the newspapers put the story on their front pages. BLOOD TEST FEARS, FAMILIES AT RISK, GOVERNMENT STANDARD UPSET, the headlines screamed. The articles were no less sensational. Like the following, which began:

"New evidence that has just come to light throws doubt on all blood tests that have been in standard use to determine paternity and parentage. This effectively means that couples who have undergone these tests have no guarantee that they are not biologically related. They may even be brother and sister. The blood tests appear to have been an expensive waste of time and money ... ..."

The reporter who wanted to interview John for the television programme was persistent.

'I've got to do this story while it's still hot,' he told John on the phone.

'I've been told to run the programme with or without you. It's in your best interests to put your side of the argument,' he accosted John as he left his office.

John managed to hold him off for three more days, desperately trying to gather some more evidence in the meantime. But he could not keep the newspaper reporters at bay. Everywhere he went they followed him, bombarding him with questions.

'What will happen to all those families who depended on the results of the blood tests they were given?'

'The government is in real trouble about this now aren't they?'

'Can you give us an idea of how the law will deal with this?

The attention was relentless and unforgiving. It impinged on all of us because the reporters could not resist asking us questions too if we happened to be accompanying John, which we did more and more often to give him support. And then, when John's picture became familiar, ordinary people began stopping him to ask advice on their personal situations.

'We had the test because we were worried about this very thing happening. Neither of us knows our true parentage for sure. What shall we do?'

More and more questions arose to which there was still no tangible medical answer except the one the doctor was giving, although John was putting forward plenty of legal arguments.

JUDGES POSED WITH MOMENTOUS DECISION, a headline stated, referring to the weighty arguments that John and the doctor were presenting.

The whole family gathered in the television room of Mark's parents' house, waiting expectantly for John's appearance on television. The opening music played and the programme titles traversed the screen revealing the television studio set ready for the debate. At the behest of the producer, John had invited a scientist and a consultant haematologist on to the programme to join the debate in support of his case. The doctor had done the same. All the contributors sat around a large round table with John and his guests on one side and the doctor and his supporters on the other. The presenter sat between them.

'How young John looks, and that doctor!' Mark's mother remarked, 'and how similar they are in appearance.' The similarity was indisputable.

'They must be the same age too,' the judge chipped in, 'It's quite remarkable how sometimes people look alike, but its not often you see them sitting together. They do say that everyone has a double.'

The presenter posed some searching questions to get the discussion underway. I knew that John had prepared questions beforehand to help the presenter to obtain the best information from his invited experts. I did not know if they would be used.

'The matter under discussion tonight poses not just a legal problem but an ethical one too,' the presenter began.

He asked the doctor about his ideas first. The young man gave answers to every question clearly and forcefully, projecting his argument with increasing certainty. He was sensitive and charming and in no time had quite won me over.

John's case seemed far less clear cut. Even though his experts confirmed in a most vehement fashion that current opinion in the law and medicine supported John's argument, he had difficulty holding his own in the face of the doctor's personal experience.

'There can be no doubt as to the validity of my argument. I can find no-one who is able to disprove it,' the doctor spoke confidently as his contribution drew to a close.

'Well, the final verdict will be left to the court. Let us wait and see what transpires there,' John was given the last word.

CHAPTER 16

Ten days later the court was convened in a blaze of publicity. A bank of newspaper cameramen and television cameras were positioned outside the court building monitoring the arrival of all the key players in the case. The courthouse itself dwarfed the proceedings. It was a magnificent old building that embodied the best architectural features of its age, a time when no expense was spared to beautify important establishments and no trouble was too great to ensure its lasting usage. The doorways held huge heavy oak doors surrounded by intricate carved work depicting scenes from ancient legal battles. Statues of famous lawyers were installed on raised platforms at first floor level on either side of a stained glass window. John told me afterwards that when seen from inside, this window cast multicoloured light onto the vast stone staircase that dominated the back of the entrance hall. Because it was such a high profile case, permission had been given for the proceedings to be televised.

Once again the family gathered around the television set, this time in our own home. The television cameras panned around the courtroom setting the scene. Three large, grand but uncomfortable looking wooden chairs each with a crest of arms at the pinnacle of its back were placed behind the judge's bench, which was set high above the rest of the room. The bench itself almost filled the width of the courtroom. Several feet in front of the judge's bench and facing it were rows of plain bench seating. The front of these rows of seats were graced by two wide table desks, one to the left and one to the right, with a large gap between them. The left hand table was occupied by John, while the doctor with his lawyer sat at the right hand table. The public gallery was packed with people. Everyone stood up when the judge entered the room.

'May we have the opening case for the plaintiff,' the judge requested, when everyone had sat down.

The doctor's lawyer stood up and looked slowly round the room. He made a short address to the assembly, explaining the law and the legal matter being tested.

The judge called upon the defence.

John briefly put his case. 'We will show that there is no case either medically or scientifically for changing the law with regard to blood tests based on only one piece of evidence that contradicts it.'

The proceedings began in earnest when the doctor's lawyer called the first witness.

A young man entered the courtroom and went to stand in the witness box. The court bailiff swore him in. Here was another young man who resembled John, only this time he was older.

'Please tell us your name,' the doctor's lawyer asked him.

'I am Harvey Colerin', the young man gave his answer.

'And you are the brother of my client, Dr Colerin?'

'Yes sir, I am.'

'How do you feel about my client, your brother? Do you feel that he has the same family characteristics as you?'

'Absolutely sir, he is my brother and I have always felt him to be so. We have a great deal in common, both in appearance and attitudes and I have never for one moment doubted that he is my blood brother. I and my other brothers have the same characteristics and outlook. We have never once suspected anything different,' the young man smiled broadly, certain of all his replies.

The lawyer called four more witnesses, all brothers of the doctor who each testified in exactly the same way. The fifth brother, the last to be questioned, entered the stand and gave his testimony.

' Son? Boys are not easy to bring up, my dear', 'I have five sons … .' The words of the lady who had occupied the bed next to me in the hospital where John had been born echoed in my brain.

'Josephine Colerin,' shouted the court usher.

Josephine? Josephine? Where have I heard that name before? I asked myself, even though I already knew the answer.

A well-dressed woman of ample proportions ascended the witness stand. She was older and a great deal larger, but there was no mistaking Josephine, the lady in the neighbouring bed in the hospital.

'Josephine,' I gasped.

I sat transfixed as the lawyer asked the lady a question.

Are you Dr Colerin's mother?'

Danny, my Danny always wanted to be a doctor! The memory of his often-stated ambition returned to me vividly.

My face drained of blood and I began to shake uncontrollably, muttering 'Josephine' and 'Danny' incoherently under my breath. Every one of my assembled family noticed my change of humour.

'Are you all right Ruth?' Mark sat next to me and put his arm round me, 'You look as if you've seen a ghost.'

'No, its nothing,' I wanted to answer, but distress had closed up the pathways of speech from my brain and I was unable to utter a sound. In my mind's eye I saw all the events of that fateful day when I changed over the babies replaying themselves over and over

257

again. I was in the nursery, my hand reaching for the machine that would seal the babies identity. "Good luck. Be rich, I'll always love you," I whispered tearfully as I gave my baby Danny a last kiss. Josephine was lying dishevelled in bed as she was given my Danny to feed remarking, "Have you noticed how alike our babies are?" And all the while my eyes rested steadfastly on the doctor.

'Can you give the date and place of birth of your sixth son, please Mrs Colerin?' the doctor's advocate requested.

The lady in the witness stand, Josephine, stated the name of the hospital and the date of birth of her son. They matched exactly my own baby Danny's date and place of birth. I could no longer dismiss the fact that this doctor was my son, my own Danny.

I could control my emotions no longer and my voice burst free of the involuntary shackles that had bound it. 'Danny,' I exclaimed, 'Danny,' loudly and urgently, as if he could hear me.

Everyone turned to face me and stared at me, their eyes wide in unspoken curiosity. Mark held me firmly. 'What's the matter Ruth? Who's Danny?' someone asked.

'Come and lie down on the sofa, Ruthie,' Mark led me gently to the large upholstered sofa at the back of the room, 'Here, put your feet up.' He took off my shoes and placed a cushion under my head. 'Try and stay calm,' he coaxed while I took in large gulps of breath.

'How long were you in the hospital, Mrs Colerin?' the voice of the doctor's advocate continuing his examination of the witness broke back into the room.

'I wasn't in the hospital long. There were no complications after the birth and I prefer to be in my own home. As far as I remember, I left as soon as I was able to obtain medical permission to go.'

'Now, you have stated that Dr Colerin is your son. Are you certain of this? Have you any reason to believe that he is not your child?'

'I am as certain as I can be. I have never doubted for a moment that he is my son. I know nothing at all about him not being my son or not being his father's son.' Josephine pulled at the hair that framed the side of her face in an effort to tidy it, though every hair was in place, just as it had been on the day when I saw her arrive at the hospital. She appeared entirely composed and confident. This little mannerism was the only sign that anything at all out of the ordinary was happening to her. 'I am very proud to have born all my children to my husband. He is the only man I have known since the day of my marriage. And what is more my son looks like his father and behaves like his father. People have told me that my children resemble my husband and myself in equal measures. Daniel is no exception.'

She called him Daniel! Why did she do that? How did she do that? In my agitated state, I could hardly take in what she had just said and I did not understand. But as her words sunk in I began to think that perhaps my story about Danny had influenced her in some way. The camera focussed on the doctor, zooming in to give a close up of him. I lay on the sofa shivering more and more violently and mesmerised by the scene unfolding in front of me. This is Danny! I am looking into the face of Danny, my baby Danny, here on the television screen! Can it be? How can it be? It is! Danny!

The lawyer posed more questions and the lady answered. I watched, my eyes glued to the screen, engrossed in the interchange as if I were there myself alternately putting the questions and then answering them. Only my answers were different from those of the lady on the witness stand.

John, John! I felt like jumping up and shouting aloud, I can help. I know the answers. Only I can solve the problem for you.

Yes, I knew the answers, but could I help, really? The huge reality of what was happening was only just beginning to dawn on me. All the years of uncertainty and suppressed fear were slowly coming to the fore, tightening their grip on me. You can help, a small voice told me. How can you help? Why does this have anything to do with you? A louder voice intervened, shaking me violently. You know why, the small voice cried quietly but insistently. You know nothing of the father, the mother, the loud voice became louder, fearful. You do, you can help John, the quiet voice was sobbing. Mum, you can help. John's face flashed before me. Mum, you can help. I saw Danny's face too. But how can I help? What can I say? All kinds of emotions engulfed me and I burst into floods of tears.

My father-in-law approached me and lifted me to my feet, guiding me to our bedroom and ushered me to lie down on the bed. He fetched a wet flannel from the adjacent bathroom and laid it on my forehead. Mark accompanied us, all the while explaining to his father, 'Ruth was in love with a soldier in the army before she met me. He was called Danny and he was killed. It affected her greatly then and I'm sure that the memory of him and what happened to him affects her still.'

The judge continued to look after me attentively. I closed my eyes and feigned sleep. Soon, I felt, there would be questions and these I did not want, nor could I cope with them. I was not ready to consider any discussion of my behaviour or what had caused it. Seeing that I appeared to be asleep, Mark and his father quietly left the room, leaving me to my thoughts.

I lay on the bed, my mind oscillating between replaying the scene in the courtroom, conscious consideration of my dilemma and blind panic and fear. Who is the young man? Is he really my Danny? How could this have happened? Why now? Why at all? Everything was so steady, settled, stable and happy. What on earth will happen now? But it's Danny. You know it is Danny. You've wanted to know what happened to him for so long. What shall I do? You can't do anything. You mustn't. You must not say anything. You will damage too many lives, John's life, Danny's life, ruin everything. And Mark and the family? It will break them too. How will Mark feel when he finds out you did not trust him, tell him, share with him, when he put so much trust in you? The judge will turn against you, exclude you, even support a charge against you to have you put in prison. There were no answers and I continued to lay in bed, opting out.

Days passed. I knew that I was withholding from John evidence that could help him, that the doctor was my own son Danny. Still I spent most of my time lying in bed. I did not wash or comb my hair. I could not eat. I was possessed by my dilemma, to tell or not to tell? Everyone thought that I had lost my reason. And in some ways I had gone out of my mind. Mark insisted to anyone who would listen that it was a reaction to the death of my soldier, that I was having a nervous breakdown because of that, something about the court case had triggered it, but he couldn't say why this should happen now nor did he seem very convinced himself. He was trying to find a reason for my behaviour, clutching at something in my life that he could understand and that he knew had really affected me. All my instincts were to tell him the truth, but I lacked the nerve to expose him to it.

On the third or fourth day of the onset of my malaise, my father-in-law knocked softly on my door.

'Can I come in Ruth?'

He did not wait for my answer, but entered the room silently, leaving the door ajar and drew up a chair at my bedside.

'Ruth dear,' he began in a pleasant, matter of fact tone, 'you know that as a judge I have a lot of experience of people in trouble. In all my years on the bench I have often seen those people react in just the same way that you are doing now. And it means only one thing; they are feeling guilty about something or have something to hide.' His face was kindly and his voice sympathetic, but I felt panic rise again from the pit of my stomach. I looked at him, my eyes desperate with a plea for mercy and my forehead furrowed in anguish. I so wanted to tell him everything, there and then. He recognised the meaning behind my expression and continued talking to me as he always had after welcoming me to his family, as a father to his daughter, who more than anything he wanted to help, 'Do you really think that we judges never do anything wrong or illegal? Do you think that we are all angels?'

I gave the judge a questioning glance. I had never doubted his integrity for one minute. I did not know any other judges, but I had always assumed them to be like him.

'Well, if you do, then I'm afraid you are mistaken. Judges sometimes break the law too. I'll give you a personal example. When I was a young man I was very indignant when a man came before me accused of driving while under the influence of alcohol. He had caused a minor accident whilst in that state, and although, thank goodness, no one had been hurt, I was ready to give him the maximum punishment, usually reserved for a person who causes a fatal accident or one in which someone suffers a permanent disability. But then I realised that I myself had taken the wheel several times after having a drink or two at a party or dinner at a friend's home when it was late, and I wanted to get home quickly and could not wait for a taxi. When I remembered these occasions, the correct penalty was imposed on the errant driver.'

'I did something else. I found an excellent liquor in a foreign country I visited and took a few bottles home. At the border I conveniently forgot to declare the extra bottles that exceeded my personal allowance and did not pay the tax. I've done other silly illegal things too. I am no angel and neither are any of my colleagues.'

I listened carefully to the judge's account of his misdemeanours, but could not equate them in any way with my own crime, even though I knew that any misdeed on the part of a member of the judiciary would be treated with much greater harshness than if anyone else had been responsible.

'Ruth, dear, you aren't eating, you are not speaking and you are neglecting yourself and your normal life. Please, whatever it is, tell me what is bothering you so much. You are behaving like a frightened child with all the world against you. You are not alone. We want to help if we can.'

The judge rose from his seat and approached the door to leave.

'Is telling the truth more important than protecting the name of the family? Of all those you hold dear?' My cracked voice echoed across the room, despite myself, arresting him in his tracks.

He came back and resumed his seat. 'It depends on whether anyone else depends on the truth being told. If they are waiting for it, relying on justice to prevail. If someone's life, reputation, integrity or rights would be in jeopardy if the truth were withheld, then the truth must be told. Everything else must be sacrificed for justice and the rule of law. There are very few occasions where keeping hold of the truth can truly be justified.'

'But I did something so bad that no court, no judge nor any ordinary person could forgive me or show me mercy,' I sobbed. Tears welled up inside me and overflowed. There it was out. I had admitted it.

The judge's face retained its kindly outlook, showing no sign of surprise. 'Which person who has broken the law does not think that his crime is the worst that has ever been committed? That is normal. It is only when he stands before the law to be judged that he realises how much the law and the courts understand his problem and how much they can do to help him. The law has evolved over a great deal of time and many safeguards have been instituted to ensure that it deals fairly and effectively with those who come before it. When all the facts become known, the miscreant understands that his was, after all, not the worst crime.'

The judge made me feel that he knew everything that I had done and that he was entirely sympathetic to me. I took a deep breath and began my story.

'I grew up in a very poor home at a time when there was virtually no hope of someone from my background ever making anything of themselves. I was 16 and only had my daydreams. I never considered that it would be any different. Then I met Danny, a young officer in the army and my life changed forever. Whatever I am now, I owe to him. He loved me, he encouraged me and he made me feel special. He thought that I was someone who was worth something and was capable of great achievement. I loved him and he made me happy even though I was poor. He wanted to be a doctor. We had great plans that were dashed to pieces when he was suddenly and cruelly taken from me.'

The judge listened attentively, making occasional sympathetic sounds to encourage me.

'It took me a long time to get my life back on course. In fact it wasn't till I met Mark that I was able truly to move forward and live life to the full again. In the meantime I made huge mistakes in my fumbling efforts to put the past behind me. One of those concerned my first husband, Jack.

'My first job was in the fashion department of a large department store. It was arranged for me by a lady from the local authority with whom Danny had been negotiating to try to get us moved from the broken down hovel in which we were living. I did not want to carry on at all without Danny, but she reminded me what Danny would have said and encouraged me to take the job. So even after his death, Danny was still looking out for me. The job, selling beautiful clothes, which once would have thrilled me, was just a job to me. The social life of the store's employees was busy, but I avoided all activities, and only had contact, through sheer necessity, with the girls I worked with. Only one girl endeared herself to me, mainly because she came from a similar background and understood me.

During my lunch breaks, my preferred pastime was to wander around the shopping centre, along all the routes I had frequented with Danny, remembering our time together. One day I was rudely interrupted from my reverie by a young man who worked in the store as a general factotum.

"Ruth, Ruth," he called me from behind, "Are you measuring the street?" he asked foolishly.

Jack knew about my problems, because there was so much gossip about me in the store, but he showed no sign of sympathy or consideration for my feelings, continuing his urbane chatter.

"I'm going to buy a motor bike one day and then all the traffic will have to move, vrrmm, vrmm."

"Do you want to marry me?" I asked suddenly, my voice full of ridicule. He was so very stupid.

"All the time I saw you looking at me in the shop, I was sure you wanted to tell me something," he replied with a confident smile.

I only wanted to get rid of him by saying something nasty, I did not imagine that he would not notice. Somehow the idea took hold. I decided to marry him to escape from the constant pressures that my family, friends and acquaintances put me under, telling me to pull myself together and attempt to lead a normal life. They thought that I should behave sensibly by going out and enjoying myself, finding a husband and settling down like everybody else. With Jack, the family would see me safely married and stop worrying about me. I could live as I chose, unfettered by a caring husband.

Jack, who was not the kind of person to spend long weighing the consequences of his actions or even to think it odd that I should make such a proposal, agreed, glad I suppose to have someone take an interest in him. My friend in the shop was mortified for me, but I was neither sorry not apprehensive about my future. Jack would give me a son whom I could call Danny and whom I could give all my love and raise to be just like Danny.'

'Mark has told me about the feelings you had for Danny,' the judge interjected, 'they have coloured your whole life, haven't they? But what has this got to do with your distress now?'

I nodded and told the judge everything that had happened to me after I married Jack: my life with Jack, the babies I lost, Mark bringing me the ticket, my fruitful holiday and the birth of my son.

'Mark told me about the man you met on your holiday and how he met you with baby John. I really admire you Ruth,' my father-in-law smiled at me warmly, 'In the end you challenged the adversities that faced you, grabbed the opportunities that presented themselves and made something of yourself. If I had met you, I would have married you. I am not surprised that Mark loves you so much.'

The judge's compliment stunned me for a moment and I began to cry, lost for words. The judge took my hand and squeezed it in his own. I leant forward and rested my head on his fatherly shoulder, glad of the comfort it brought me. But I still had not told him about changing the babies.

'It would not surprise me now, Ruth dear, hearing how you felt and the terrible things that happened to you, that when the baby boy, who you wanted so much, was born to you, you loved him so much and wanted so much for him to live and for his life to be good and secure that you made sure it would be better than anything you could provide for him. You did that, didn't you Ruth? You did not consider the consequences, but from that day your action has haunted you.'

I nodded slowly, fresh tears coursing down my face, truly astonished that the judge had been able to guess.

'This is not a case of such terrible proportions. You had too many tragic events to cope with for one so young. You were so wrapped up in your love and your loss that you took the only logical step for you. No one ever helped you to deal with your loss. I am sure that a psychologist will testify to the enormous emotional strain you were under. This can be resolved without too great a punishment.'

'I don't care if I have to go to prison,' I sobbed, 'I just don't want Mark or John or Gary or anyone else to suffer because of me. Do you still think that I should tell the truth?'

The judge sat quietly thinking for a few minutes.

'Do you want to meet your son Danny or are you content to continue with your life as it is and forget that he ever existed, and never to know what becomes of him?'

Emotion gripped my throat making my voice rasping and barely audible, but I managed a whisper, 'I would willingly give up everything just to spend a few hours with my son Danny.'

'Then there is only one course of action open to us,' the judge's face relaxed. Although his exterior appearance was always impassive to the casual observer, I had noticed a certain tension since my initial outburst that I realised now stemmed from his concern for me. 'This evening we will tell all the family what has happened. Then we will contact a registered therapist and take the matter to the court. We will tell the judge your story to see if he thinks that it will help the case.'

I felt the blood drain from my face as fear rooted itself in my brain. I still could not bring myself entirely to trust the judge and now he was talking about putting the matter before someone else.

The judge noticed my apprehension. 'Don't worry,' he said, 'I'll be able to sort out almost everything. But I must warn you that when we tell your story, the police will be involved and they will do all in their power to arrest you. They may be able to detain you in a police cell for a while, but it won't be for long. We will get bail for you until it's been dealt with.'

As the judge spoke, I continued to stare at him, my eyes wide and my face pale and drawn. The feeling of panic tightened its hold on me.

'You will not be able to talk to anyone except your lawyer and the police will make your situation look very black. They will accuse you of the most severe charge available to them and tell you that you face a very long prison sentence. But Ruth, they only know what you did. They do not know your circumstances or what your defence will be. You must tell them the absolute truth.'

When the judge finished speaking, I was more determined than before not to reveal the truth. The consequences terrified me. 'What if my defence is no good, if you can't help me?' I asked, afraid that he and Mark would desert me.

'Ruth, I know how hard this is for you,' the judge attempted to mollify me, 'you've spent years thinking that we would abandon you if ever we found this out. It's still hard for you to trust anyone. You probably still are not sure of us.'

How does he know? That's exactly how I feel, I thought.

'But this is exactly how they will want you to feel and they will play on it. They will tell you that we are no longer interested in what happens to you and that you have no-one to help you. They will urge you to sign their own prepared confession. If you do that, then we really will not be able to help you.' The judge took both my hands again and looked at me with genuine affection, 'Ruth, I want you to know that I love you, as Mark does, and that we will stand by you.'

My expression remained fixed in a tight frown of fear and trepidation. I was unconvinced.

'All right, Ruth, I am going to tell you something now that I have never revealed to another soul, so that you can understand how much I trust you and love you and so that you will trust me.'

Where I was fearful and reluctant to admit my error, the judge did not hesitate. He was determined to gain my trust even if there were to be a personal cost.

'Many years ago a young girl, who had been caught stealing a bra from a large store, was brought before me. The normal sentence at that time was 40 days. In court the defence insinuated that she had taken the bra for someone else and the defence lawyer submitted this in mitigation. But the prosecution managed to prove that the bra size was an exact fit for the girl herself. When I questioned the girl, she broke down and told me that she needed the bra because she didn't have one. "But why", I asked her, "did you not claim money from social security to buy one?" "What do you mean, social security?" she replied. Then I realised how innocent she was and sent her away with a warning never to do it again. That lunchtime I came across her, drinking coffee in the court cafeteria. I sat down with her and so began a romantic liaison that has lasted until now. She bore a son by me. He's grown up now, a bank manager. But nobody knows of my affair and thank goodness there has been no breath of scandal.' The judge paused for a moment to give his revelation time to sink in. 'So you see I do truly understand you and I can assure without any doubt that I will be with you whatever happens.'

I held my head in my hands and sighed deeply, then looked up into the eyes of my father-in-law, knowing that in this man I had no better friend or confidant in whom I could place my trust.

That evening everyone gathered around the family dining table for our evening meal. Everyone but John, that is, because he was working late, as usual. Mark's father sat at the head of the table and indicated that we should all be silent.

'My dear family', he began solemnly, 'We have all seen how upset Ruth has been of late. Now I have managed to persuade her to tell me what has been worrying her.'

They all nodded and looked attentively at him.

'I am afraid that what I found out will be shocking and upsetting, but poor Ruth has had her reasons, as will become clear.'

As he proceeded with the narrative, each person present reacted in their own way, but only my mother in law showed that she did not understand me. She rose from her place at the table, muttering crossly, 'This is madness. You must have been quite mad. How could you?' and left the room.

'Yes, I was mad after I lost Danny,' I admitted quietly as she left, though I don't think she heard me.

Mark sat stock still in shock. I knew that he was finding it hard to take in what his father had just told him and that he must be terribly upset that I had kept such a secret from him for all these years. Yet, he took my hand and held it firmly until he had composed himself enough to speak.

'Ruth, I want you to know that I respect and admire you for telling the truth now and facing up to the problems ahead.'

After Mark spoke, nobody felt it was their place to say any more and we all sat in an uncomfortable silence for a while, broken only by the occasional cough or sigh from Gary and Victoria who alternately smiled at me awkwardly and looked into their laps.

'Oh mum, it must have been awful for you,' Victoria finally broke the silence.

'A friend of a friend of mine was killed in a road accident,' Gary chipped in, 'his mother went completely to pieces.'

When everyone had had time to absorb the situation and the atmosphere resumed an air of calm, we set about discussing how we would tell John.

CHAPTER 17

John arrived home and without taking time to take off his coat, hurried straight into the dining room where we were all still assembled.

'Take off you coat John,' his grandfather commanded kindly, 'and then come back and have your dinner.'

John made no attempt either to leave or to sit down. He had something weighty on his mind that could not wait.

'I can't carry on,' he blustered, 'I'm going to ask to be released from this case. I've done everything I can think of, but its no use.'

'Just a moment, lad,' his grandfather broke in calmly, 'Sit down now. Your stepmother may be able to help you.'

John's eyes darted curiously around the table and he sat down heavily on the nearest chair.

'Stepmother! Why did you say stepmother?' he cried in astonishment.

'Ruth, you had better tell him.'

'I love my mother. I don't know what you are talking about,' John protested fervently and without hesitation.

His display of utter love and faith caused tears to engulf me again and I was unable to utter a word. It took me ten minutes to compose myself enough to speak. Slowly and carefully I related the whole story of my life to him. In my highly charged emotional state the story telling took some time, as I had to pause each time I came to a tragic event. When I reached the part where I changed the babies, tears began rolling down John's face. He got up and put his arms round me, 'Mum, oh Mum,' he wept, cuddling me ever tighter to comfort me.

When he eventually released me, I looked round. Everyone present had tears in their eyes too.

'John, I'm not your mother,' I tried to tell him, but he put his finger up to my lips.

'Please mother, I never want to hear you or anyone else ever say that again,' he said, kissing my cheek.

Mark also could not restrain his tears. Now we were all crying together, John, Mark and me, and everyone else too. Only my father-in-law was smiling, happy to see how devoted we were to one another and how much we loved one another. Nothing would be able to break the family apart.

The moment John put his finger to my lips, I realised for the first time that I felt closer to him than to anyone else in my life. I put aside consideration of any baby who could come between us and take his love away from me, or my love away from him.

'John, do you know that because of you all my luck changed for the better?' I told him lovingly, 'I believe it was you that brought me the good luck that altered the course of my life.'

'I'm so glad Mum. It's a great pleasure for me that I could do that for you,' John smiled broadly, 'I won you and you couldn't get rid of me. You don't know how lucky I feel too that you are my mother.'

We embraced each other again, like a real mother and son.

'Mum, one day I will tell my brother Danny that too,' he laughed, 'I want the film cameras to be there when I break the news to him, so the whole world can share our happiness.

John went to the beautiful old walnut drinks cabinet that his grandparents had given us and took out a bottle of champagne. 'I am supposed to keep this until I am seventy years old,' he explained.

'But you aren't seventy,' I protested.

'No, I'm not, but the person who gave it to me was fifty and I am older than twenty, so I consider the time has been served. Besides, he told me to keep it for a special occasion and I cannot imagine any more special occasion than this.'

'Please John, don't open it yet. There will be a more special occasion I promise you,' I insisted.

By now, everybody was smiling broadly, all happy to be members of our loving family. My mother in law, who had returned to be with us when we greeted John, came to put her arm round me.

'Well, well, I had no idea that people lived like that,' she said, reminding me of something else Josephine had said, "Did people really live like that?" She was innocent of life too and that was another reason why the judge was so impressed by me.

John had left the house long before Mark and I rose the next day. Even with all my revelations, he still did not possess the answers that would help him to solve the case. I slept late, released at last from all the pent up stress of the last days and years. Mark was sitting on the edge of the bed next to me when I awoke.

'Darling Ruth, I want you to know whatever happens how very much I love you. Every day that gives me a chance to know you better, I love you more.'

'Even if they put me in prison for ten years, will you still love me and wait for me then?'

'What do you mean?' Mark's expression changed from tender to quizzical.

'I may get a very long prison sentence for what I did.'

'Who told you? Where did you get that information?'

'Your father, but he did say that it wasn't likely.'

Mark immediately took up the telephone that stood on the bedside table.

'Hello, may I speak to Dr Breake please?' Mark tapped his fingers rapidly on the small table while he waited to be connected. 'Ah, Dr Breake, this is Mark, Bella's son.' I was so used to Mark being referred to in connection with his father's name that I was surprised to hear his mother mentioned now. 'I am so sorry to disturb you so early, but I have a really serious problem that I must discuss with you urgently.'

From the part of the conversation that I could hear, I realised that Mark was talking to a psychiatrist who had seen his mother at some time.

'We can be there in an hour. Yes, you'll see us then? Oh, thank you very much.' Mark replaced the receiver with a relieved sigh. 'Come on Ruth, get dressed. There's no time to lose.'

'But Mark, I'm not sick. I don't need a doctor.'

'He's not a medical doctor, he's a psychiatrist, the best in town and you have to meet him urgently. He will tell you what to say.'

Well, that's a turn up for the book, I thought. Mark has made exactly the same suggestion as his father.

'You know, you should have been a lawyer,' I laughed, 'You think just like one. Why didn't you go into the law?'

'Because I don't like the way the legal system works,' Mark looked perturbed and paused for a moment as if reconsidering a former decision in the light of current events, 'You may have to defend someone you know is guilty or prosecute someone you know is not. And sometimes an innocent person has to plead guilty when there isn't enough evidence, just to get a reasonable sentence.'

At the psychiatrist's office, we found that Mark's father had anticipated our arrival and was sitting comfortably waiting for us in the anteroom. He filled us in with some details of what we should expect when it was our turn for a consultation, demonstrating to me that he knew a great deal about the process. This obviously was not his first visit. An odd idea passed through my mind. Was it not ironic that most of the rest of the family appeared to need a psychiatrist and now I was joining them?

I sat in the smart wood-panelled office, looking at the myriad of certificates that hung on the walls boasting qualifications from and membership of every medical organisation that I had heard of and many more that I had not. There was a painting too, which had been given pride of place, of a very wise looking old man in old fashioned clothes. I recognised the name 'Sigmund Freud'.

The psychiatrist's secretary emerged from his room. 'Dr Breake will see you now,' she said, ushering us in to see him.

Dr Breake was much younger than I had imagined after looking at the painting outside. He was rather thickset in stature, but had a comforting, almost jovial face that immediately made me feel at ease. He shook hands with each of us and then waved his hand towards three identical pale blue upholstered chairs in front of his desk.

'Please sit down.'

Mark held out the middle chair for me to sit on.

'Well, Ruth,' Dr Breake began, looking me straight in the eye, 'Your father-in-law has filled me in on most of the details of the problem, so I only need to ask you a few other questions before we proceed.'

I returned his gaze expectantly and nodded.

'Are you sorry for what you did, Ruth? Are you willing to apologise publicly to the court, to the hospital and to the other family and take responsibility for what you did?'

I sat still for a moment, contemplating the events of the last few weeks, considering my relationship with John and the huge amount of luck that he had brought me.

'No, I am not sorry, not a bit,' I replied out of ignorance and innocence. There was no doubt in my mind, knowing the outcome now, and forgetting the years of fearfulness, that I would have done it again.

'If that is what you feel, Ruth, it will help you in court. But not in the way you would imagine or wish.' Dr Breake leaned forward across the desk, as if to give me some very intimate and confidential information. 'The prosecution will suggest that you did not know what you were doing. They will say that you are not of sound mind and that you should be confined to a mental institution until such time as you realise and admit that you did something wrong. In your current state of mind, they will insist that you present a danger to society.' Now he leaned back slowly into his comfortable high backed leather chair. 'So, Ruth, I must ask you again, do you feel guilty or embarrassed about what you did?'

'No, I'm not embarrassed,' I persisted, with a half notion that I should retain my stance.

'Are you truly saying that you are not embarrassed for causing pain and upset to John and Mark and the rest of your family. That you are not worried that you have allowed John and the doctor to endure so much confusion and headache and taken up so much of their time and that of the courts?'

At last I understood his point. But once again I had to decide whether or not to tell the truth and indeed what was the truth I was to tell.

We travelled straight to the court from the psychiatrist's office. It was so much more impressive in real life than it had appeared through the lens of the television cameras. I was even able briefly to admire the wonderful stained glass window for myself as we passed through the great hallway to the corridor outside the courtroom. There we met John, who was standing talking animatedly to some of his team.

I did not recognise any of the people John was with and looked around to see if I could see the man who I thought was Danny.

'Hi, Mum, Dad, Grandpa,' John made his excuses to his colleagues and came over to us, kissing me on the cheek, 'Look, I've asked for an adjournment while we look into the new evidence. The judge has given us until this afternoon.'

I wanted to ask him where the doctor was, but felt awkward. Now's not the right time or place, I reminded myself. John must have read my mind.

'I don't know why, but the doctor hasn't arrived yet. He can't have known there would be an adjournment. I have only just asked for it.'

How are you going to solve this now? I felt like asking, but realised that it was a silly question. If John had known, he would not have had to ask for the adjournment.

My father-in-law disappeared towards some offices at the end of the long corridor. Some minutes later he returned, accompanied by a policeman in uniform and an older man in a dark suit who carried a small briefcase.

'Ruth, this is a police officer who would like to interview you and Mr Farthing, our solicitor. He will look after you.'

Mr Farthing smiled at me confidently.

The policeman stepped forward, 'Please can you come with me madam,' he requested politely.

I followed both men along a maze of corridors and up some stairs until we reached a small interview room. I hope someone takes me back, I thought. I'll never find the way myself.

The policeman sat on one side of a table by the wall and I sat on the other with the solicitor. The policeman asked me questions about who I was and where I lived and filled in my answers on a form that he had in front of him.

'I am just going to call some detectives to talk to you now,' he explained when he had finished writing.

While we waited, Mr Farthing told me what would happen next and gave me some hints on how to conduct myself during the interview.

'You must, of course, tell the truth,' he said, 'but if you are uncertain about anything, look at me and I will deal with it for you.'

Both detectives looked very young and inexperienced, though one was obviously more senior than the other. I knew that I should not be fooled by appearances. These men were probably the brightest recruits, which was why they had achieved plain clothes' status so quickly and been entrusted with the most responsible jobs. The older one interrogated me, while the other wrote notes. A recording machine was switched on to ensure an accurate record.

The questioning was meticulous. No detail of my connection with the hospital was left out. I was required to identify every small detail of the layout of the maternity ward and the nursery and to describe the people I had met there. They made me replay the act of changing the babies again and again, to ensure that my story remained consistent and that I was not making it all up. The questioning made me feel small and stupid. They tried so hard to find out if I was mad that it was hard to maintain in my own mind the fact that I was not. The solicitor did his best to ameliorate the harshness of the interview, but his soft words and calm reassurance could not prevent my imagination from going into overdrive.

I saw myself standing alone in the dock, a high wooden bar all around me hemming me in, as the judge pronounced sentence. I imagined myself being handcuffed to a female warder and almost dragged from the building. At the door, a huge sack was thrown over my head, as a safeguard from the prying lenses and flashes of the newspaper and television cameras that were waiting outside. But it could not safeguard me from the sounds I heard out there as they shovelled me roughly into the waiting Black Maria. "Bitch", "whore", "child stealer", "lock her up and throw away the key", all kinds of people yelled, their voices filled with anger and venom.

The interrogation seemed to last an eternity, but eventually after what must have been about two hours, I was released from the dark stuffy room and returned to the airy corridor where Mark and his father waited for me. Lunchtime was over and the court was in the process of reconvening. I just had time for a refreshing cup of coffee and a sandwich that Mark had brought for me, before the court usher arrived to take us into the courtroom.

The scene inside was exactly as I had seen on television, but in real life it seemed much smaller than I had imagined and I was unprepared for the dim lighting and the slightly musty smell that accompanied the oak clad, old fashioned chamber. John was standing in front of his desk, while the doctor and his advocate sat behind theirs. Josephine was sitting in the front row of the public benches. She looked directly at me as I entered, but showed not even a flicker of recognition. I was about to sit down next to Mark and his father in one of the middle rows when the usher guided me to a recessed seat at the base of the witness box.

One of the plain clothed detectives who had been interviewing me entered the room and approached the judge.

'Your honour, we would like permission to arrest the witness and detain her while we prepare the case against her.'

Fear gripped me, until I remembered what the solicitor and my father-in-law had both told me.

'Will the witness please rise,' the judge announced. The usher indicated that I should stand up.

'Are you prepared to be a witness in this case, whether or not you are charged?' the judge addressed me.

'Yes, I will be a witness and give evidence to the best of my ability,' I replied.

The judge took a piece of paper from the detective, signed it and returned it to him.

'I am giving permission for you to be held under arrest until all the enquiries are complete. In the meantime, you will remain here in the court as long as you are needed. You may go back to your seat.' The judge made his pronouncement in a matter of fact manner, as if arresting me would have no effect on me.

'Your honour!' John stood up to protest, 'I must …'

'The defence council will sit down. This matter is not for discussion,' the judge reprimanded, leaving John no opportunity to alter his decision.

I returned to sit next to Mark. The doctor looked at John and his team and then at us in confusion, as if to say, what on earth is going on?

John rose to his feet and addressed the doctor's lawyer, 'My friend, I need your client to enter the witness box now.'

'What me, now! I don't understand,' the doctor interrupted.

'You will understand. It will all become clear,' John retaliated firmly.

'Gentlemen, this is not the way to continue. Please approach the bench.'

The judge consulted with John and the doctor's advocate in an undertone. Then John returned to his place and the doctor assumed the witness stand.

I did not understand where the line of questioning was leading.

'We need to be sure of the procedures you used to do the blood tests and the relationships between the people whose blood you took.'

'But we've been through all this before,' the doctor demurred, looking even more puzzled.

'Nevertheless I need you to confirm some important facts.'

'Please tell the court exactly what the blood tests showed about the nature of the relationship between yourself and your father.'

'Our blood groups match perfectly. We did the test several times. They proved conclusively that my father is my natural father.'

'And what did the blood tests showed about the nature of the relationship between yourself and your brothers?'

'Again, our blood groups match perfectly. They proved that all my brothers are my natural brothers.'

'Now tell us what the blood tests told you about the nature of your relationship with your mother.'

'The blood tests showed conclusively,' Danny stated with a sigh, 'that my mother is not my natural mother. The blood groups showed no match at all.'

John continued his questions in the same vein and the doctor continued to argue. I felt like shouting at him to listen and answer, but the sedate and formal atmosphere of the courtroom warned and prevented me from drawing attention to myself. Instead I rested my arm on the back of the bench in front of me, lay my head on my arm and closed my eyes in an effort to dissipate the pressure and nervous tension that oppressed my brain.

'Thank you, that will be all. You may leave the witness stand,' I heard John say.

'Call Mr Colerin,' summoned the court usher.

There was a long pause, presumably while the witness made his way to the box. The witness was sworn in. I kept my head in its comfortable position on my arm.

'Mr Colerin, you are Doctor Colerin's father?'

'Yes I am, as far as I know. I was in no doubt at all until all this business blew up.'

The voice, that voice! I pricked up my ears and listened intently.

'Did you ever have any reason to believe that he is not your son?'

'No, not at all. He is like me in more ways than I can say. More even than any of my other sons. He has my looks and my character traits.'

The sound of the voice echoed loudly in my ears, then pounded into my brain. I know that voice. I know that voice!

I looked up and there sitting in the witness box was Nelson, whose voice I had recognised. Nelson? What is he doing here? Is he Josephine's husband? But this means … . Is he saying that he thinks that Danny is his son, really his son. And I had changed one of his sons for another. The thoughts in my mind were weaving round and round themselves. I could not take it all in.

John approached the bench again and asked the judge something quietly.

'Mrs Colerin, would you mind leaving the room for a moment?' the judge asked Josephine.

When she had left, John addressed the man in the witness stand.

'Do you recognise that lady?'

I started as John pointed to me. Nelson looked at me hard for a few seconds and answered in the negative.

I'm Ruth! Don't you remember me? That wonderful holiday we spent together. Don't you remember that? I stared at him, hanging on to this little bit of certainty while I struggled to come to terms with the implications of the new revelations.

'Please. Mr Colerin, look at the lady again. Take your time. I must remind you that you are under oath.'

'Is my answer very important, whether I know that lady or not?' Nelson looked confused.

'Sir, we are trying to solve a most perplexing problem. We are not accusing anyone of anything, but it is extremely important that you identify the lady if you can.'

John was at his most persuasive and despite the situation, I felt proud of him.

'Her face looks familiar, I must admit, but I cannot place it.'

'May I ask the court's permission to jog the witness's memory,' John directed his query towards the bench.

'You may. Go ahead,' came the judge's reply.

'Let me remind you of a business trip to Spain that you took in the year before your son Dr Colerin, was born. You met a young lady on your way there.'

'Oh my G ...' Nelson's countenance changed completely as realisation dawned, 'Yes, oh yes,' Nelson raised his hand to his head and scratched it rapidly. He looked at me again, this time with recognition. 'Is your name Ruth?' he asked.

Still dumbstruck, I could only manage to mutter my reply.

'Please can you speak louder so the court can hear you,' the judge's voice reverberated around the room.

'Yes, it is,' with great effort, I managed an audible answer.

There was a huge synchronised intake of breath from the benches where the public sat and then the courtroom burst into uproar. Each person was in loud discussion with his neighbour or the person in front of him or the person behind her, 'Did you hear that?' 'You know what that means.' 'Who would have thought it?' A couple of reporters rushed out. The judge had to bang his gavel heavily on his bench to gain anyone's attention.

'Quiet please! Order! Can we continue!'

'Do you remember the romantic liaison that you had with this lady?' John repeated to Nelson.

'Yes, I do now.'

But Danny stood up and shouted in confusion, 'I don't see how this is relevant.'

'Sit down!' the judge ordered, and again called John and Danny's lawyer to his bench. When they returned to their places, Danny's lawyer whispered something to him. Danny went pale with shock.

'Now I can reveal to the court the reason why there has been so much confusion in this case,' John stood forward confidently, all his hard work at last vindicated as told his own story. 'Ruth bore a baby as a consequence of that romantic holiday, in the same hospital as Mrs Colerin. Her baby was called Danny, after a soldier who died, but she swapped him for Mrs Colerin's baby. By a huge coincidence, both babies were fathered by the same man – Mr Colerin. This explains the strange and unorthodox results of the blood tests. The father was indeed the same man, only the mothers were different.'

Chaos erupted. People jumped up from their seats and began pushing along the rows to get out. Others shouted to each other. A camera or two flashed and the people who had left the courtroom were replaced by a crowd from outside trying to get in. This time, the judge banged and banged his gavel but it had no effect. Court bailiffs, ushers and other personnel were summoned to quell the disorder, to no avail. Eventually, the judge gave up and called for an adjournment until the next day.

John and Danny embraced each other, brothers recognised at last. I watched them together, as if their reunion was the most natural thing in the world. I was happy, but I did not run to Danny, nor did I attempt to hug him myself. I felt totally drained. All the excitement that I should have been feeling could not rouse me into taking more than a passing interest.

Then by common consent, on a tide of movement, I was swept out of the courtroom into the long corridor, which was heaving with people and activity. Mark and his father tried to keep next to me, but we were separated by the enthusiasm of a throng of reporters determined to have their story.

'Ruth, why did you change the babies?' 'Are you sorry now you changed your son?' 'What does John think?' 'Who was Danny?' 'Why did he mean so much to you?' The only way that they would let me have any space was to answer their questions and this I did quietly until Mark and his father rescued me, almost lifting me bodily through the horde who pushed and pulled at us, until my father-in-law guided us to the safety of a room near the judge's chambers.

They kept me in a police cell for one night while Mark and his father sorted out the huge amount of bail money that the police had requested. The cell was small and bare except for the bench on which I was expected to sleep and a blanket. I looked around me and mused on the turn around again in my fortunes. I had begun my life in simplicity and with next to nothing. Would this be how I continued it, in a prison cell, for goodness knows how long? Still, at least this place was dry and warm. I would bear it. I had my family to support me now.

The next day the newspaper headlines were unanimous about what was the most important story. Mark was allowed to visit me and brought a batch of papers with him. LAWYER AND DOCTOR – LONG LOST BROTHERS, SWAPPED BABIES HAD SAME FATHER, WHAT A COINCIDENCE!

The court was reconvened later that morning with no less interest and fuss than on the previous day. A female police officer accompanied me to my seat in the dock. I surveyed the courtroom from my lofty position in a tall high, box-like podium structure that placed me just below the level of the judge's bench. The place was packed and terrifyingly, it seemed that everyone was staring at me and whispering. The judge would not enter until decorum reigned. He eventually took his place in a hushed and expectant silence.

'Any interruptions today will be dealt with most seriously,' he began, 'if there are any outbursts like yesterday, I will clear the public gallery completely.'

The judge called my name and the police officer told me to stand up. Now, at last was the moment I had been dreading. My fate was to be announced.

'You will be pleased to know that all charges against you have been dropped. The injured parties have declined to press charges and there is not a strong enough case against you, after all this time, for the state to prosecute.'

An audible sigh rippled through the courtroom, but the assembled crowd remained otherwise quiet, remembering the judge's admonishment.

'However, it would not be proper of me and I would be failing in my duty if I did not advise you, most strongly, that your conduct in this matter has been extremely irresponsible. We understand that you were very young and vulnerable when you committed this iniquitous act. But today you are a well respected and upright citizen. You should be ashamed to have put your family and your son's family through the heartache and agony they have undoubtedly suffered and to have so wantonly wasted the taxpayer's money. You allowed this trial to go on for much longer than it needed to.'

I bowed my head in recognition of what I had done.

'I am very sorry, your honour.'

'The case has now been formally resolved and the government vindicated. You are free to go. The court is dismissed.'

Everyone rose to their feet as the judge left the room. Before I had time to draw breath, Mark had grabbed my hand and whisked me speedily along the corridor and out into the fresh air. The steps outside the building were crammed with people, most of whom wielded huge, complicated looking cameras, all pointing at me. As I emerged, voices called to me 'Ruth! Here Ruth!' I hid my face in the large scarf that Mark had brought for me that morning for just this eventuality. Somehow, we managed to reach a taxi that took us straight to Mark's parents' house, where we had been invited to stay until things settled down.

My story claimed media attention for several days. Every reporter was looking for an original slant on the story or trying to obtain an interview from us. As soon as they began to run out of steam, some unpleasant accusations began to be made.

MOTHER ABANDONS SON AGAIN, SON REJECTS MOTHER WHO DESERTED HIM. This last was most disturbing. I wondered, is this something that Danny has told them? The idea upset me greatly. Once again I could not eat or sleep properly. I did not know what to do. It still did not feel right for me to contact Danny after what I had done to him.

CHAPTER 18

On the third morning after the end of the case the telephone rang.

'Hello Mum,' it was not John, but the voice sounded very familiar. The voice was Danny's voice, Danny my soldier.

'Mmm, it's, it's Ruth,' I stammered. Tears hovered in my throat blocking my voice.

'Mum, I understand why you did what you did. You did it for me,' Danny sounded cheerful and expectant, 'I want to meet you, as soon as possible.'

'Mmm, yes, I want to meet you too,' I said, stifling my emotions so that I could reply, 'You can come here at any time.' I gave him the address of my parents in law.

'Is tonight all right? Say seven o'clock?

'Yes, yes, of course. See you then.' I put down the phone and cried buckets.

When I finally composed myself, I hurried downstairs to the kitchen. The kitchen maid stopped me as I reached the doorway. She held a single flower in her hand wrapped in a white bow.

'Excuse me madam, this just arrived for you.'

It was a large orange marigold, my favourite flower, the flower that my soldier Danny always bought for me. A card hung from the ribbon "To Mum, With Love from Your Son Danny".

I cradled the flower in my arm and contemplated the card in my hand.

He has come back to me. Finally he has come back.

The telephone did not stop ringing. John rang first.

'What's happening Mum?' I told him that Danny was coming. 'Well, if you don't mind, I want to meet him too. What time did you say?' John, in his usual hurry, replaced the receiver before I could reply.

Mark rang and then Gary and Victoria. Somehow everyone knew that something was happening. Of course it was John who told them. Danny must have asked him for my number. But what surprised me most was a call I received early in the afternoon.

'Ruth? It's Nelson,' his voice was confident and happy, 'I'm sorry that … .'

'There's nothing to be sorry for,' I stopped him, 'you made my dream come true.'

'Ruth, I am so glad to hear you say that. It's been a lot for us to absorb, but we know that Daniel wants to meet you and we wondered if we could come too.'

I realised that Danny must have invited him, in the same way that John had invited himself. The young people were taking over!

'Yes, of course, I'll be delighted to meet you again.'

'Well, its not just me who wants to come. All my five boys would like to meet you too.'

'Yes, that's fine. The more the merrier,' I replied, glad that we were at my father-in-law's house and not our own. Where would we have put everyone?

'Just a moment, Ruth, Josephine wants to speak to you.'

'Hello Ruth,' before I could protest or worry, Josephine greeted me, 'I hope you don't mind if I come too. We must compare notes on bringing up boys. Do you remember the advice I gave you in the hospital?' She did not sound angry or threatening, just polite and understanding, a mother sympathising with another mother.

I arranged for everyone to come at 8 pm.

An hour before the rest of the family, Danny arrived. We hugged each other at the door, clinging tightly together for a long time. Then, even before I took his coat, I folded my hands around his hands and took a good look at his face. His features were just like mine, same eyes, nose and mouth, but his colouring and hair were Danny's. When he turned round to remove his coat, there was the distinctive curl in the nape of his neck, just like Danny's.

We had all his life to catch up with, but for the time being, we were content just to sit together, comfortable in each other's company.

The party, with all our family present was as happy as a wedding. John opened his 'seventy year old' champagne and we all toasted the future. As we lifted our glasses, John stood on one side of me.

"This isn't the end, my love."

Danny stood on my other side.

"I will come back to you."

I distinctly heard the words echoing down the years. Danny had kept his promise. We celebrated our wedding all together, surrounded by happiness and love.

Books to follow from the same author:

Pearls of the Sages — a collection
of moral short stories

The Reluctant Guerilla

Noah's Ark in our Time — an
entrepreneur saves millions of
people from the atom bomb

The Other Side of Hell